MW01228117

A STORY OF SORROW

Book 2: The Unburied

Daniel J. Volpe

Bad Dream Books

This one is for Robert Jordan.

BOOK 2: THE UNBURIED

CHAPTER 1

The mouth of the cave looked like a monster from a child's bedtime story, but to Dorak, Shelbren, and Mur, it looked like salvation.

The driving rain pelted the three scouts, soaking through their oiled cloaks like they were thin cotton. A flash of lightning sizzled in the air, followed immediately by a roar of thunder. It was getting dark, even darker with the blowing storm, and the temperature was dropping. High on the mountain, the weather was a fickle bitch and could kill at will. Especially those that weren't prepared.

The three scouts, members of the eighth regiment of forward observers, thought they were prepared, but found themselves in trouble. The rain had started as nothing more than a light shower; not bad, considering the hike had been grueling. Soon after the rain, the wind picked up. And then the thunder and lightning, followed by an outright deluge. The men braved the storm, determined to reach their objective, and return home.

The mountain was simply known as the Borderlands. It was craggy and littered with patches of scrub brush. The trees, what few there were, had been stunted by the lack of water and near-constant winds. Still, the Borderlands was an important barrier between the nations of Tarbent and Bulharo.

For generations, the two territories had been tense, with a few skirmishes here and there, but all-out war was never waged. Small raids were conducted from time to time, but those were usually personal, not dealing with the nations themselves. Neither country laid claim to the mountain range, and it sat as a neutral territory; a stone giant watching over them, keeping them apart.

The scout's tasks weren't anything overly complicated: reach a vantage point, observe the base of the Borderlands at the border of Bulharo, and return home. Simple, or so they'd thought.

"We need to get into the cave!" Mur yelled over the blowing storm. His cloak pulled and snapped, and he fought to keep the hood down.

The other men agreed but only answered with nods. There was no use yelling into the storm.

Slowly, and gently, the men trekked across the rocky terrain, careful to avoid any areas of wet moss.

The cave wasn't much, but it was a refuge, and for that, the men were grateful. The opening was low, too low for any of them to walk upright. They crouched and entered, feeling a wave of relief to be out of the pounding storm.

"Fuck," Shelbren said, unshouldering his pack. It was soaked through, but he hoped his fire kit was dry. He tossed off his cloak and shook the water from it. His hands were chilled, but not yet numb. Wet, cold clothes clung to him, and he knew if they didn't get a fire going, they'd freeze to death.

Dorak and Mur followed suit. They were equally wet, but they were seasoned scouts. Remaining calm was the first part of survival, and panic would only rush them through death's door.

By the light of the storm, the men sorted through their packs. Between the three of them, they had a dry fire kit.

"Motherfuck," Mur grumbled, scratching his knuckles with the striking steel. He hit it again, throwing a shower of sparks onto the tinder. The flames sputtered and caught, feeding on the dry material. They carried little for fuel, but each man had oil-soaked chunks of wood and cloth.

"Ah, that's much better," Shelbren said, warming his hands in front of his small fire.

Mur and Dorak did the same, but they knew without a larger fire, they could still be in trouble.

"Not much in here," Dorak said, looking around the dark cave. His small flame was balanced on a flat rock. He picked it up, casting orange light around them.

The other men looked, knowing there wasn't much to see.

"We're going to need some wood and a much bigger fire if we're going to wait out the storm," Mur said.

"Agreed, but where in the blue fuck are we

getting dry wood?" Dorak looked at the ceiling of the cave, hoping to find some old roots hanging down. The light danced, penetrating the gloom. He moved deeper inside, listening.

The sound of rushing water echoed through the cave. He moved towards it, not seeing the source. The ground was dry, but the water sounded like a small river. The cave ended. At least it appeared to.

"Find anything good?" Mur asked. He hadn't moved from his flame, but he was watching his fellow scout explore the cave. It was what they did; explore. Looking for the lost, the unknown. It was in their nature, which was why they'd signed up to be scouts.

"Nah, it just sounds like a damn river in the wall." He put the flickering flame near the wall and realized there was a crevasse he hadn't noticed before. It was long and thin, and hidden unless you stood in just the right area. "Actually, I think I did." Dorak didn't look back at his friends. The temptation of an undiscovered location excited him. He felt like he did the first time he'd laid with a woman. This was a different slit, but equally dangerous, he was sure.

"What is it?" Shelbren asked as he stood. He pushed his flame onto a stone as well and picked it up.

"Fuckers," Mur grumbled, following his two friends.

"I'm not sure, but this thing goes quite a ways." Dorak held his light in front of him. The urge to rush forward was nearly unbearable, but he held fast. If he hadn't, he wouldn't have seen the glittering chips overhead. "The King's arse," Dorak said, raising his light higher.

Mur and Shelbren had caught up to their friend. Their eyes shot up, looking at the glittering ceiling above them.

"Sweet fuck," Mur said, holding his flame higher.

The ceiling sparkled like the clear night sky. Gems and shimmering veins of gold lined the rocks above them.

They stared, and shockingly, they weren't as cold as before. They were still wet, but the excitement of their find was enough to put the threat of death out of their minds.

"It just keeps going," Dorak said, following the riches overhead. He walked, not watching where he stepped. "We'll be heroes for this discovery." Thoughts of riches and the women they'd bring clouded his mind.

Mur stepped up next to him. "Hey, listen."

Dorak snapped out of his reverie, leaving the scantily clad women in his brain. "I don't hear anything."

Shelbren stood with them, straining his ears. "Me neither."

"Exactly," Mur said. "The water. It stopped."

Dorak looked like he'd swallowed something sour. "How in the fuck is that possible?" He looked around, expecting to see a silent river. "That's just not possible." He walked further into the cave. A shiver ran down his spine, but he didn't know if it was from the cold.

Mur and Shelbren moved up with him, each man holding their shaking flames ahead of them. The cave continued and cut back a few times, but still, it ran further.

"I think we're done," Shelbren said. "The cave looks like it ends," he peered into the gloom. "Let's go bac—," he stopped. His flesh was covered in goosebumps and his head snapped towards the darkness.

The sound of the river was back, but it wasn't water they were hearing. It wasn't water they'd heard in the first place.

It was breathing.

The three men looked at each other. Their pale skin shone red in the weakening firelight. They didn't blink, nor did they breathe.

Dorak took a cautious step backward, away from whatever awaited in the darkness. His wet boots slid across the stone floor, kicking a rock off the wall, and to him, it was painfully loud.

He froze, his heart in his throat. The breathing sputtered and deepened to a growl. Something moved in the inky darkness, something large. Something with claws that clicked on the stone.

A three-fingered claw on an impossibly long arm shot from the shadows. The long, wicked nails dug into Dorak's left thigh, sinking to the bone.

"Fuck!" Dorak fell to the ground, blood rushing from his leg. He looked back at Shelbren and Mur, making eye contact with them. "Help," he muttered, feeling the arm tense up.

In the blink of an eye, Dorak was gone, pulled into the darkness. His flame lit up the horror in the shadows before it was snuffed by a gout of arterial blood.

Shelbren was already gone, running blind into the blackness towards the opening in the cave.

Mur stood there for a moment, which was probably a moment too long. The monster, it was the only word to describe it, was massive. In the flash of light, before the flame was snuffed out, he saw more than enough. It was like the afterimage one got from staring at the sun, but it was forever stamped in his brain. He couldn't describe it and never even attempted to. Even when questioned by the King's men, he couldn't do it. He only would say one thing: it had teeth.

A lot of teeth.

CHAPTER 2

The alley was dark and stinking of fish, but it didn't stop Fesha from sucking the man's cock. She squatted in front of him, making sure her skirts were out of the grime. With skills long since perfected, Fesha slurped, hoping to finish soon. One hand followed her mouth along his wet shaft, while the other held his thigh for support. The man tensed, a sure sign that her job was almost over. Which was good. She'd been working all night and her jaw was throbbing. Faster she sucked, making slurping noises that always seemed to hurry them along. The first salty glob hit her tongue and Fesha shoved his cock as far down her throat as possible. It wasn't her favorite taste in the world, so if she could bypass her tongue and send his seed straight down her throat, even better.

The man was almost on his toes as the last bit of cum was deposited down her gullet. Slowly, he relaxed and shivered. Fesha didn't know if it was from the cool night air or her oral skills.

"Alright, love, that'll be twenty coppers," she said, standing. Her knees popped, and she wiped her mouth with the back of her hand. The man, a young man with dark features, tucked his wilting cock away. She didn't know why an attractive man, such as he, would pay for a street whore, but she didn't mind. Work was work, and he was probably the cleanest customer of the night. When she'd first seen him, Fesha hoped he'd want a fuck, but that didn't happen. Regardless, she couldn't afford to become pregnant again, so a suck was better in the long run.

The crash of the sea in the distance was dull. A sliver of moon was more than enough to chase away some shadows lurking in the alleyway. And more than enough to reflect on the blade in the man's hand.

Fucker's gonna rob me, Fesha thought. For a moment, she considered reaching for the blade she kept in her stockings, but knew she wasn't fast enough.

"Now, look here. This is dirty business," she said.

The man grabbed her throat with his free hand, crushing her windpipe, and slammed her against the rough brick of the wall.

Fesha saw stars when her head cracked into the plaster. The man punched her in the stomach repeatedly. A warmth ran down her belly and into her crotch.

Not punched, stabbed. He's fucking stabbing me.

The knife flashed in the moon's light, piercing whatever flesh it could find. Fesha faltered. Her weak kicks and blows had done nothing to stop the attack. If anything, it spurred the man along. She clawed, trying to reach his face with her long, dirty nails. Fesha hooked a chain around his neck, pulling forth a shimmering amulet from his shirt. The metal was mirrored finish and, in its reflection, Fesha glimpsed fear in her eyes.

It was the last thing she'd ever see.

The whore fell to the dirty alley floor. Fin followed her down, letting his knife work. Her blood ran free with every unnecessary stab, but he wasn't ready to stop—not just yet. He never learned her name, nor did he care. She served a purpose—actually, two purposes. She gave him one of the finest suck-jobs ever and, for the time being, quenched his bloodlust.

The skin on her face yielded to his knife, as the honed tip popped her dead eye. Fin pushed it deep, burrowing it into her brain. Pulp and fluid seeped from the hole. His jaw throbbed—he didn't realize he'd been grinding his teeth since the attack began.

Raucous laughter echoed down the alley. Fin snapped his attention towards the street as another whore and a customer came stumbling down. The whore—*his whore*—looked up at him with a red eye and a bloody smile. Fin smiled back, wiped his blade on her dress, and ran.

The streets weren't crowded at this late hour, but quite a few people were out.

The city of Ayr contained one of the largest ports in the known world, holding ships from every nation. Men and women from all walks of life. Some of whom made their living in the darkness of night, trading ill-begotten goods. It was the perfect place for Fin and the men aboard the stolen ship. Anonymity was key, not only for a man with his peculiar tastes, but for Sorrow and the others. It wasn't in every city where Church items could be sold and sold discretely. Ayr had that reputation. A city of freedom, of opportunity. A city where no vice or fetish was looked down upon and where

11

everything had a price tag.

Fin passed a drunkard pissing on the side of a building. He stunk of urine and cheap alcohol.

"Spare a copper, yung'in," the man slurred. He turned towards Fin, nearly hitting him with his acrid stream of urine.

Fin's hand went to his sword, which was under his cloak. He could feel the dampness of the whore's blood on his clothing, but he was careful not to soak himself again. He rather liked his outfit and cloak. It would be a shame to discard them. This time around, he opted for a black cut, which helped blend the gore.

"If you even so much as hit my boots with your piss, I'll slice your cock off and shove it down yer throat," Fin said. His hand itched to draw steel. He wanted to run the vagrant through, relishing the feeling of his sword entering a gut. Fin wished a blade would materialize in the man's hand, making the murder justified. Eyes were on them, but none of them was the city watch. Part of him thought he could kill this man in the street and no one would raise an alarm. Who in the blue fuck would care if a drunkard was killed? It would be one less rapist and mugger off the street, and the bone saws would have a fresh corpse for their dissections.

The old bum looked at Fin, taking in his glare.

"Eh, fuck'ye then," he grumbled. The vagrant put his cock back into his pants, but had yet to finish his piss. Fresh urine darkened the fabric as he stumbled away to harass others.

Fin's nose wrinkled at the sour smell left behind, but his ears perked up when a scream pierced the night air.

His whore had been found.

CHAPTER 3

They'd been in Ayr for four days and had already sold off most of the Church's belongings.

Sorrow walked out of a jewelry shop, with Jagrim in tow. The purse on Sorrow's hip was much heavier than when they'd walked in. Pickpockets —mostly dirty children—watched them. Sorrow tapped the purse with his hand—the tattooed one. A young boy, no older than eight, looked at the snake tattoo as if the man was crazy. There came a sharp whistle from one doorway and Sorrow watched the ringleader, a boy of maybe twelve, run his fingers across his neck.

Sorrow smiled. In Ayr, even the thieves respected a blade master. Especially one with steel so obviously displayed. Sorrow had yet to find himself a better sword and didn't think he would. The blade at his hip and the dagger on his waist were more than sufficient. He wasn't a snob, needing a handguard as twisted as the hair on his crotch. No, just a long, sharp piece of steel that wouldn't break. When he saw men with polished swords full of gilt, he knew they were easy marks. They wouldn't fight, and if they did, he knew they'd die quickly. It was rare to see a true killer with a fancy blade.

Jagrim stepped up next to Sorrow, watching the little vagabonds scatter, searching for their next mark. "Aye, the cheap fuck didn't even give ye full price on some of that Church shit."

Sorrow shrugged. "I wasn't expecting him to. You," he tapped Jagrim on the chest," and I are clearly no men of the cloth."

Jagrim grinned, splitting his red beard. "Hey, speak fer yerself. I am a man of honor and dignity." He couldn't even finish the statement without laughing. Jagrim's stomach growled, loud enough to be heard over the din of the lively street.

"Let's spend some of this coin on lunch," Sorrow said.

"Aye, I won't fight ye on that."

The business district of Ayr was busy, especially at midday. Many ships that had docked that morning or night before were unloaded and ready for trade. Merchants, along with their guardsmen, walked the streets in fine clothing. Most of them rode in small carriages or were carried in palanquins. Wagons loaded with crates, live animals, and tarp-covered goods clogged the cobbled streets. Beasts of burden bit and shit, creating a dangerous and repulsive roadway. Even so, the city functioned properly. And for a city— and especially a district such as that—to function properly, food was a must.

Stalls and carts had been set up along one of the wider streets and in a small square. The smells of the combined food were strong; a rich tapestry of culture. Voices of different languages yelled, trying to be louder than their neighbor. Food of various shapes, colors, and smells rose high from baskets and pots.

Sorrow and Jagrim stopped and surveyed the display in front of them.

"Any of this interest you?" Sorrow asked.

He was looking around at the different foods and people. It looked like the entrance to the fighting pits, except no one was scheduled to die after lunch. At least, he hoped.

"Aye, it all looks good." Jagrim leaned in close. "Especially the women."

Sorrow nodded. "Yes, some comfort is needed later." His stomach growled. Not nearly as loud as his friend's, but more than enough. "But I need to fuel up before I have a run at a whore."

Jagrim didn't look at him, but nodded. He was still scanning the offerings. "No good taverns? I could use an ale to wash down whatever I eat."

Many of the buildings had hanging signs, but in this part of the city, he didn't think they'd find an established eatery. And then he saw the sign with the overflowing mug. "There," he said, smacking Jagrim on the chest.

"Perfect," Jagrim said, but he'd already started towards the building.

The tavern wasn't crowded, which was a plus. Most of the merchants either supped with clients or had food aboard their carriage. Their men and the laborers didn't have the time, nor coin, to sit for a midday meal.

Sorrow and Jagrim took a small table in the corner. A cold fireplace was next to them, but the other tables were empty. The only other patrons sat at the bar with plates of sausage in front of them.

The bartender, a drab woman of middle years with gray-streaked brown hair and a dirty apron, walked over towards them.

"Wha' can I getcha?" she asked. There was a permanent scowl on her face and a hand on her hip.

Sorrow didn't take his eyes off her. He smiled at her. It wasn't a condescending one, but a genuine one. He'd aged well, not quite the looker he was at Fin's age, but he was never called ugly. Sorrow's black hair was finally clean and pulled back in a stubby ponytail. Even his unruly beard had been trimmed and shined with a light coat of oil. He put a thick silver coin on the table and watched the bartender's eyes go to it.

"Good afternoon, my dear. My companion and I would love some of your finest ale," he looked at Jagrim, who was nodding, "a *pitcher* of your finest ale and some lunch. Whatever you're serving is fine. We are not picky eaters."

The bartender's hard veneer cracked, just slightly. She bent down and grabbed the silver coin, slipping it into her apron. "Aye, comin right up," she said, this time with just a little less venom in her voice.

Jagrim watched her skirts swish as she walked away. "She'd be a fun one to roll around with."

"She'd eat you alive," Sorrow said. The food and drink came quickly, but the tavern crowd didn't grow. Both men ate and drank in silence, watching the people pass by through the window.

Jagrim belched, covering his mouth with the back of his hand. "That was a fine meal. Nothing to it, just good cooking." A plate with small bones and a few crumbs sat in front of him. His mug was nearly empty, and he refilled it from the pitcher.

Sorrow nodded in agreement with his friend and gestured for the man to top off his mug as well. "Cheers," Sorrow offered, raising his cup.

Jagrim touched his to Sorrow's. "Cheers. To forbidden magic and the deep pockets of the Church." He gulped his drink, leaving suds on his red beard.

Sorrow drank, but was slightly more reserved

than his hulking friend.

Yes, cheers to the magic indeed. Without the blood magic Sorrow had stolen so many months, even years, earlier, they'd all be dead. Or worse, mindless zombies serving the necromancer. And yes, part of him had to give thanks to the Church. Even though things didn't quite end well for Vicar Prentas, the man saved Sorrow's life on the beach. And the more Sorrow read the man's private journals, the more he understood his fight against agents of evil.

"And have the opinions of the men changed at all? It's easy to be grateful when something happens, but time is a bitch to the mind. You, as well as I, know that comfort can make memories hazy." After Sorrow had incinerated the necromancer and his flesh hulk, he'd known it didn't sit well with some men. When he slaughtered Brother Kirsh and Vicar Prentas, he thought he was going to have to fight a few of them on the beach. They weren't stupid, regardless of their faith. Even exhausted, Sorrow was a killer. A few of them could've overwhelmed him, but many would've died. And no man wants to be the first in a suicide charge.

Jagrim drank again. "Eh, the ones that had issues have departed. They took their forged bank notes and left. More'an likely gonna get picked up by another outfit here, or join up with a merchant's guard."

"Maybe they'll join up and head to the Borderlands," Sorrow said.

Jagrim nodded. "Aye, that's quite possible, too."

Since landing in Ayr, word of the fighting in the Borderlands was on everyone's tongue. The two nations had been at each other's throats since the dawn of time. Stemming from an ancient family feud that no one could seem to remember, they were sworn enemies. Most military tacticians would wax and wane on which nation was the stronger of the two, but neither had committed to full-scale war in generations. A mountain range, rightfully named the Borderlands, separated them. For years, this natural barrier kept the fighting to a minimum. Until recently. As Sorrow knew, blood follows money and when money is found, blood flows.

Ayr wasn't very far from the fight, making it a perfect hub for mercenaries to link up and traders to find bodyguards. Trade, either in steel, spice, or flesh, followed war, and the dregs of Ayr were more than willing to provide all three.

Sorrow wasn't much interested in fighting for either side. He didn't give two blue fucks about the right to the mine, but the headhunting was simple work. The other fools, the young killers, could wet their steel with fresh blood. If he had his choice, he and his men would swoop in after the carnage and collect a few heads. Clashing steel, while he'd never shy away from a fight, wasn't the only thing on his mind. If it had been a decade or two ago, young Sorrow would've been more than happy to wade into battle, seeking to end lives. And ending lives was his specialty.

"Do you think any of our men want to fight?" Sorrow asked.

Jagrim looked at him over his mug. "Eh, I'm sure some wouldn't mind wetting their blades, but most of them are just interested in wetting their cocks. We're mostly an older bunch, Sorrow, looking for the easy money, not the bloodiest."

That sounded great to Sorrow. The fewer pointy things aimed at his heart, the better. But one thing stuck in his brain. Something he hadn't been able to shake. It was as if his mind was a fresh pair of wool trousers and he'd walked through a briar patch. As hard as he tried to pluck the uncertainty from his consciousness, it held fast.

"Aye, that may be true for most, but what of Finleos?" Sorrow asked.

Jagrim filled his mug with the rest of the pitcher. He didn't look at Sorrow until the foam rose to the top of the earthenware.

"Aye, that boy," he looked up at him, "that boy is different, alright." Jagrim sipped, slowly. "He's one of the best, even without the experience of older men, but ye seen it, Sorrow. He lives to kill, that one. Now, don't get me wrong, there's nothing better than a good swing of the axe and the feeling of it cleaving your enemy down, but if I could get the same purse to hawk turnips, I would." He lifted his beard along his jawline, revealing a pink scar. "Most turnip farmers don't have to worry about curved blades trying to take their heads off."

Sorrow contained his laughter at the thought of Jagrim, the turnip farmer. Some men are built for murder and he was one of them.

"Have ye heard him in his sleep?"

Sorrow shook his head. "Can't say that I have."

Jagrim drank. "He talks. A lot." A drop of foam fell from his mustache onto the table.

Sorrow shrugged. "It's not uncommon, especially for men specializing in wet work, like us. You're telling me none of it haunts you and comes to you in the dark?"

"Aye, aye, of course I see it; some of it, at least. And I'm sure I grumble here and there, but Fin *talks* in his sleep. It's almost like he's having a conversation with his demons."

19

Sorrow had spent many years sleeping next to others. People, when they entered their dreamland, weren't themselves. Most would toss and turn, mumble things in their slumber, and even shriek. They were all different. And yes, a few of them would often have talks with their minds.

"I've heard worse," Sorrow said. "What is he speaking of? Confessions, secret lovers?"

"That's the thing. I've never heard a word of it, just the tone of his voice. Even if he's in the next tent, it still sounds like the boy's underwater." He grabbed his mug and upended it. "Anyway, his sleep-talk isn't doing anything for me." Jagrim looked out the window. "We've been here for a while, wouldn't ye say? Just a bunch of chatty cunts."

Sorrow let out a small laugh.

"Let's head back to the inn and divvy the loot." He paused and put a finger up with a smile. "*Most* of the loot."

Sorrow had already skimmed some when he was paid, but he would not protest a little more. He'd done the killing, anyway. Plus, the Church was *going* to come for him, that was certain. Having some extra coin to grease palms couldn't hurt.

The men stood and Sorrow put an extra silver coin on the table.

Jagrim adjusted his axe and rubbed his full belly. "I'm definitely full, but I have another craving that needs satisfaction." Ayr, like many larger cities, had its fair share of whores. Many of them were the streetwalkers, giving a quick back-alley suck-job, or hiking their skirts up for a fuck. A few houses offered higher-end women, mostly foreigners and women or men with peculiar fetishes. Those were not the women Jagrim was looking for.

"I'd have to agree with you, my friend. It's

been too long since I wet my cock." The two men walked back out into the swarming street and headed towards their rooms.

CHAPTER 4

Night had fallen, and the city was alive.

If Fin had his way, one less person would be alive in the dreadful city. After killing the whore the night before, Fin was planning on lying low. He had considered even heading to the theater district and possibly taking in a show. But that would cost coin, and why spend coin when he could kill for free? The look on the whore's faces was better than any performance ever. It was genuine, even if their lust towards him was not.

Fin wanted to stalk the docks again, but knew better than to kill in the same spot. It wasn't his first time cutting up a woman of the night. If anyone had followed his path along the world, mutilated prostitutes would be his marker. The docks were easy thanks to the swarm of fresh bodies. Most murders and robberies were often unsolved and if they were, a foreigner who didn't speak the language was often found at the end of the noose. But Fin was smart.

The business district was full of merchants, traders, and workers completing legitimate business by day, but at night, they were hunting for more than a bargain. The wide thoroughfare was lined with hastily erected stalls and carts. Each of these offered a delicacy, whether it was food, drink, women, men, tobac, or the stronger, more potent, kesh weed. Fin cared not for intoxicants, at least then and there. To feel his blade enter flesh, the last few pumps of the dying heart shivering on his knife; that was his drug.

Women yelled to him, some from the open windows above. None of them were right. Too public, and he certainly didn't want to pin himself down in a room. Nothing good could come from that. Too many eyes on him, watching him enter. His cloak had done well with hiding the blood splatter and the washwoman—whom he'd wanted to stab in the face—did excellent work. Of course, for an added fee, she would ignore the blood stains. In the city, many fights occurred and blood was spilled, mainly by drunken men. If she only knew the truth…

Fin stalked, pushing away lude offers from garish whores. No, they weren't right. He'd know the right one. His knife would tell him.

There! His brain shouted. He was calm moments before, but now his heart was a stampede. She was perfect. The older woman she was standing with—presumably her mother—was arm-in-arm with a drunken man.

Fin pushed through the crowd, never taking his eyes off her.

If the girl was over fifteen, he would be shocked. Pox scars dimpled her face and her left eye had a slight droop to it. The lumps in her chest were a clear indication of stuffing and her short nails looked bit to the quick.

The girl watched her mother disappear into the crowd, heading towards a group of men standing in a doorway.

Fin was locked on her like a shark smelling

blood. His push through the crowd was met with many curses, but most men weren't out for a fight. Another predator had made the girl his target, too. Fin watched the fat sailor pushing through the opposite side of the crowd. The big man wore a shirt that was too small and covered in brown stains. Greasy hair poked out from the brim of his low hat and his eyes were sunken. A dagger was tucked in his belt; a blade that looked far too expensive for the likes of the man.

The girl saw the sailor moving in on her and was looking for a place to run. Fin was just a step too late.

"Eh, there, girl," the fat man said. He grabbed her thin arm in his wet palm, holding her tight. "You looking for a good fuck?"

The girl looked at Fin, who stood watching the encounter. A look of pleading, along with fresh tears, was in her eyes.

"Aye, a fuck'll be fifty, good sir," she said. Her nose wrinkled at the odor wafting off the man.

"Fiddy? I wouldn't pay more'en fifteen to stick me pecker in a little whore like you. Pox scars and fake tits." He grabbed at her padded chest and pulled her in close, trying to whisper. She turned her face from his but couldn't escape his hold. "Maybe I'll take my fuck for free. Just to show you a good time. Maybe you should pay me," he spat.

She shuddered. A tear fell, running down her bumpy cheek.

The sailor glanced at Fin from the corner of his eye but said nothing. Fin cleared his throat and still went ignored.

The whore looked at Fin with tears in her eyes.

Fin cleared his throat again, this time much louder, and took a step closer so he was within arm's length of the pair.

"And what do ye want, boy?" the sailor asked, no longer able to ignore him.

"I already had a date set up with this young lady," Fin said. He pointed to the young girl with his hand. "I made arrangements with her mother for her services, and I intend to collect on that."

The sailor let go of her and looked him up and down. His hands were large and calloused, tipped with dirty nails. He didn't reach for the blade at his waist, but his beady eyes shone with frustration and anger.

"Find yer own whore," he said. "Besides, you look more like a fairy, anyway. See if one of the fellas can give yer pecker a suck." He took a step closer—a little too close.

With nimble fingers that had lifted a purse or two as a boy, Fin plucked the dagger from the man's belt. The weight of the blade was surprising, but didn't slow him from hiding the knife in his cloak.

Fin took a step back. This wasn't out of fear, but the stench wafting from the man was wretched.

"Listen, you fucking oaf," Fin said. Gone was the softness of his voice. "This girl is mine. Get it, mine. I will cut your pathetic cock off and stuff it down yer throat, if you take another step."

Some bystanders slowed to watch the confrontation, which was the last thing Fin wanted. Being seen with the girl was a risk, but drawing attention was even worse.

The sailor smiled. His teeth were the color of mud. "Oh, yeah?" the sailor asked. His hands went to his belt, looking for his dagger, which hid in Fin's cloak.

With a quick movement of his arm, Fin pushed his cloak back, revealing his sword. "Friend, don't take my appearance for weakness. I'll spill yer fucking guts on the street and sleep like a babe." Fin didn't draw steel, but the twitching in the back of his hand showed he could at any second. "There are plenty of whores. I suggest you find another."

The resolve had melted from the sailor like a lump of tallow in a pan. He looked back at the girl, who'd taken the opportunity to move closer to Fin.

"Eh, fuck the both of ye. A nasty skank and a fairy. You'll make a great couple," the sailor barked. He didn't even ask about his knife, which he'd probably stolen, anyway. He turned and pushed his way through the crowd in search of another poor soul to harass.

Fin covered his sword and belt knife—not the one he'd stolen, but the one he'd soon be using to carve up the young prostitute.

"No one has ever done something so nice for me before," the girl said.

Fin was watching the sailor but knew the man wouldn't give him any more trouble. At least that night. He hardly noticed the squeaky voice next to him. Fin turned and looked down. The whore was against him, and her arm was snaking through his. Her breath was sour and had the slightest odor of semen on it.

"Hmm?" Fin grunted.

She wrapped his arm tight and stood on her toes. "What ye did. Chasing that oaf away. It was the nicest thing anyone's ever done for me." She batted her eyelashes at him. Her cheeks were worse up close, caked with makeup that was clumping.

Fin started walking, knowing she would move with him. He patted the back of her hand with his, stroking her cold skin. "It was my pleasure," he said. The alley was ahead, calling to him to enter the darkness. To step into the gloom and commit murder. Under the silver moon, he'd spill innocent blood. Fin's cock was hardening—not at the thought of sticking it in the young girl, although that would happen first—but plunging his blade into her. Fucking her with his knife.

"My normal rate isn't fifty for a fuck. It's twenty-five, but for you, I'd gladly do ten." She giggled. "Hell, I'd do it for free if my mother wasn't expecting a cut." Slowly, leaving the crowded streets behind, they entered the darkness of the alley. "Either way, we're gonna have us some fun."

Fin smiled in the shadows. His fingers reached under his cloak and stroked the handle of his blade. Yes, they were about to have some fun alright.

The men were rougher than Aliss expected them to be, but their coin was hard and plentiful. She staggered out into the street. Her disheveled look garnered a few glances and sneers, but no one offered any kind of help. In Ayr, especially in the business district, the girls were expendable.

Aliss tucked a strand of hair behind her sore ear and looked for Yony, her daughter. She wasn't in their usual spot, so hopefully she had a date. The girl, even with her pox scars and lack of tits, was still a good earner. Men, and some women, liked them young, and the girl had been alongside her mother for almost a year. It would've been sooner, but the pox was still a little too fresh. Even the scars scared some men away. In the dark and with some heavy powder, they disappeared. At least enough for most customers, some of whom were drunk.

The street traffic was thinning out, which was

fine by Aliss. She didn't think she could handle another date that night and might have to stick to sucking pricks for the next few. When Yony finished up wherever she was, they'd head back home and hopefully not get robbed on the way. It was part of the game, especially for two women that didn't have a bodyguard to protect them. Ayr wasn't the worst city in the world, but with the number of people, there was bound to be some death.

She'd heard stories of a few working girls found dead, one of which was just the night before. There was some competition amongst the streetwalkers in Ayr, but there was plenty of hard cock for all of them. Certainly not a shortage of those. A girl close to the area had been carved up badly, her face destroyed by a knife. What was even worse was the fact it wasn't believed to be a robbery. And that wasn't even the first. Another girl, this one by the docks, had been found gutted and floating in the harbor. Now, this wasn't uncommon to find someone in the water. Stowaways, mutineers, and pirates were sometimes killed and dumped. Drunkards were usually the ones found in the seawater, with their faces half-eaten by fish and skin sloughing off from the salt. And yes, the occasional woman was found murdered. Those were often crimes of passion, a jilted lover returning home, or sometimes a dock whore found killed. It was part of the job, a hazard they all had to accept.

Aliss made her way over to the last spot she'd seen Yony. It was their meeting spot. She shivered and hugged herself. Her top was ripped, and buttons were missing, so she had to hold it closed to maintain some level of modesty. Not that she cared, but she wasn't looking to attract anyone else that night.

The moon was high, peeking out from behind some of the taller buildings. Aliss stamped her feet to ward off the creeping cold. "Where the fuck is she?" she asked aloud.

Many dark alleys lined the street. More than likely she was down one of them, but Aliss didn't know which. The last thing she wanted to do was to disrupt the girl at work. That was never good for business. But it was getting late, and she desperately needed to wash.

Damn it, girl. If you can't make a man shoot his seed with this much time, I've certainly failed you, she thought.

A rotten stench entered Aliss's nostrils, causing them to wrinkle. She turned and saw a bloated, greasy sailor lumbering towards her. Her sex immediately went dry, even with the remnants of the other men still leaking from her. If she'd eaten that night, she would've had a difficult time holding back her gorge.

"Ye that little slut's whore monger?" the sailor slurred. The front of his shirt was taut and wet.

Aliss wanted to back away and lie to him, but it was no secret the two of them were in the same spot almost every night. "Aye, I know the girl."

"Ye need to teesh her some fecking manners." He drank from an unmarked bottle, letting a few gulps drip down his wattle.

"I'll be sure to mention it to her," Aliss said. "But where exactly is she?"

He belched and wiped his mouth with the back of his hand. "Aye, the dumb cunt blew me off fer some pretty boy." He burped again and stopped, swallowing whatever came up with it. "They went down the alley," he pointed towards a couple of shops with alleys in between them. "Tell her I'm coming back tomorrow night and she'd better be ready for a real man." He unceremoniously grabbed his crotch and walked away.

Aliss looked toward the alleys. She had a good idea which one Yony would be in. One shop was a tailor, and they'd often toss scraps of fabric in the alley. The clumps of material would invite rats and mice, but it also made a perfect rest to kneel upon.

She was cold and sore and desperately wanted to get home, but she couldn't leave her daughter behind. The moon hung fat in the sky, creeping across it ever so slowly.

"Fuck it," Aliss said. She stopped outside of the tailor's and peered through the glass. The shop was locked up tight, but the outside lantern still burned. She took a pin from her hair and picked the rudimentary lock holding the flickering light in place. Aliss, with the lantern in hand, entered the alley.

No alley in Ayr smelled good, but this one wasn't usually that bad. Aliss had been on her knees or against the wall a few times down there. But that night it stunk. She couldn't quite place the stench, but it certainly didn't smell normal. Most of the alleys were used as toilets by men and animals alike. Street cats would bring kills back to the darkness, sometimes running away in the face of a greater predator, leaving their kill to rot.

The flickering lantern dispelled shadows as she moved further. Aliss tuned her ears for the sound of sex—either sucking or fucking—but heard nothing.

"Yony," she whispered. Silence.

As Aliss moved deeper into the alley, the smell worsened. Her skin rose in goosebumps, but it wasn't from the cold, it was from the smell. She knew that smell.

When she was a girl, her father had a farm. Once, every so often, he'd slaughter an animal either for them or for the market. Those days, Aliss had been tasked to help him and the smell of spilled guts never left her memory.

Yony lay just outside of the light.

"Yony?" Aliss shrieked, moving towards her daughter. Even without the light of the lantern, she could see the girl was dead. And by the looks of it, died horribly.

Yony was topless. The rags she would use to stuff her chest were soaked with blood and discarded. Her chest, her bare chest, was a crisscross of deep cuts and the buds of her small breasts were gone. Wet offal glistened in the torchlight. Bile and shit stunk as it steamed in the night. But this wasn't a clean cut like on the farm, no, this was pure butchery. Yony's pale belly looked like it had been ripped open by a desert cat. Knife marks were deep and violent, with no ceremony to them.

Aliss fell to her knees—splashing in a puddle of her daughter's entrails and gore—and screamed.

CHAPTER 5

The night was growing old. Sorrow and Jagrim had only accomplished losing some of their coin in a fixed dice game. Almost all the women were arm-in-arm with a man or surrounded by a few burly ones. Each time Sorrow and Jagrim approached what they assumed to be a working girl, they were promptly turned away. Twice they were met by men ready to draw steel.

"What in the blue fuck is going on with these ladies?" Jagrim asked. He leaned against a wall and pulled out a stubby pipe. With a fat thumb, he stuffed it full of tobac and lit it with a match.

Sorrow watched the thinning crowd as it passed by. It was late, too late for him. He had no intention of searching for a fuck all night, and it didn't seem like it was happening. Maybe the next day they could take a walk to a different part of the city and see what the atmosphere was like over there. But for the time being, the business district was dead.

The windows of the tavern they'd had lunch in earlier were alight. Even in the distance, Sorrow could see figures moving inside. Sorrow tapped Jagrim and pointed down the street.

"Thirsty?"

Jagrim smiled with the pipe clenched between

his teeth. "Aye, if I can't fuck, I might as well have a drink." He puffed away as they walked.

The tavern wasn't full, but there was a crowd. The table they'd eaten at earlier was taken, but a few spots at the bar were open.

"What can I getcha?" the bartender—the same one as earlier—asked. She looked up at them and realized who they were. Her dour approach changed, reminded of the coin they were throwing around earlier. "Back so soon?" She grabbed two mugs and began filling them from casks. Frothy beer crested the top as she held them in one hand. With the other, she wiped spilled beer from the bar top and set the glasses down.

Jagrim, this time, set a coin on the bar. He picked up the mug closest to him and drank. "Aye, we were out looking for," he smiled, but with a hint of shame on his face, "some…"

"Girls?" the bartender finished for him. "I've been in this city almost my whole life. Trust me, you're not the first one to want to fuck. Besides, men who stick their cocks in a warm hole are less likely to stick a blade in one of my customers." She looked up and shrugged. "Well, usually."

Sorrow sipped his beer. "It hasn't been going so well for us tonight," he said. "Seems like we have the pox or something. The girls have clammed up or disappeared."

The bartender took an empty that another patron had set down and put it under the bar. "Aye, it's been a bad few days for the ladies of the night," she said.

When they docked the stolen Church ship, the harbor and docks were teeming with sailors. And it was no secret that sailors, when they finally reached port, were looking for another type of harbor to slide into.

"Really? It seems like the sailors and merchants, especially this close to the docks, would keep them busy."

"Aye, that's the problem. From what I hear, business is good for them. But a few of the girls were lax, not working in pairs or being safe. One of these new fellas took advantage of this."

"Cheap fucker raping them? Or robbing them?" Jagrim asked.

"No, killing them," she said. "And not nicely. Although, is there a nice way to murder someone?"

Sorrow had seen many men lose their lives and yes, there were merciful ways to kill.

"He's a fucking butcher. Mutilating them, cutting their breasts off, gutting them. The worst imaginable."

Sorrow had known men like that. He'd killed men like that as well. They were predators, through and through, but they killed only for enjoyment. Some of them went under the guise of soldiers slaughtering villages after a raid. Those were disguised as the fever of battle and to send a message to all who would stand against them, but Sorrow knew. He knew the blackness of those men. The same ones that would get enjoyment from raping a man's family in front of him, before putting them all to the blade. Tactics like that weren't new. He'd even watched it happen many times before, letting it transpire in front of him. Just like being marooned on the beach, Sorrow had the will to survive and, in those situations, drawing steel would've led to his death as well. And any man, woman, or child will tell you, being on the pointy side of a sword is always a bad idea.

Sorrow drank half of his beer, leaving the rest

of it untouched. He set a handful of copper on the bar next to his mug. "For your time." He stood up and adjusted his sword. It felt good to bear that weight once more. For too long, he'd gone unarmed, and he vowed to never let that happen again.

Jagrim looked at his friend, who was signaling the night was over. He wasn't a man to leave behind a drop of beer. With a few deep gulps, he chugged his down and followed Sorrow into the streets.

Fin had stripped off his bloody clothes. The young whore had leaked like a stuck pig, and he'd gotten more blood on him than he'd wanted to. He sat on his bed in a clean shirt, with his soiled cloak and shirt in a sack under his bed. He'd have them laundered in the morning, but for the time being, his focus was on the knife he'd swiped from that fat pig of a sailor.

The lantern wasn't turned up to the max, but the blade shimmered. When Fin had taken it in, the weight threw him off. He'd held many blades in his young life and knew what to expect from a belt knife. At first, he thought maybe it wasn't a knife, but some kind of cudgel with a knife-like handle. Now, looking under the light of a flame, he knew he was wrong.

Silver. The blade was handcrafted from pure silver and not cheaply made, either. He knew he wasn't the first person to steal that blade, as the fat sailor didn't buy it himself. The firelight danced on the wall, reflecting from the edge, but another light, one brighter and not nearly as natural, joined the dance.

Fin's eyes snapped down to the amulet around

his neck. He sheathed the blade and checked the lock on his door. Fin pulled the amulet free and held it in front of his face. The light danced on his flesh, and he smiled.

The inn was quiet. The common room was dark, with just a few low-burning lanterns alight. Sorrow left Jagrim at the door, as he was packing another smoke. The inn wasn't the best, but it was clean. The owner, a hard woman from Saldrak, didn't allow smoking or whores in her building. Her bullish figure and firm resolve were not something any of the men wanted to deal with.

The hallway at the top of the stairs wasn't very long, but contained a few closed doors. Most of them were occupied by the men from the ships. Gortul, Than, and Fin had rented space at the inn, while Zakkas chose to stay near the docks, where he said the food was better. Even wearing his boots, Sorrow was quiet. He walked the halls with his key in hand and stopped. A muffled conversation was coming from a room—Fin's room. Sorrow didn't have a timepiece, but he knew the hour was late. Almost to the point of sunrise. The young man hadn't been out with them, and he'd thought some were staying put for the evening. Sorrow smiled, thinking maybe Fin was testing the inn's rules on whores, but he paused. Another voice could be heard, but it sounded odd. Almost as if they were in a cave or underwater, not standing only a few feet behind the door. Then he remembered what Jagrim had said about the boy talking in his sleep. Full conversations during his slumber, but this time, he didn't sound like he was alone. Sorrow pressed his ear to the door, and the floor creaked.

Fin's voice cut off immediately.

Like a thief in the night, Sorrow backed away and slipped the key into his lock. Just as his door latched behind him, he heard Fin's opening. Sorrow listened, but didn't hear any approaching footsteps. His tattooed hand rested on the pommel of his sword—an involuntary reaction. At least, he thought.

CHAPTER 6

The mist hung in the crags of the mountain. Wet air clung to everything, making the men's armor glisten. It would've been picturesque if not because Sergeant Werd and his men were freezing. He and his men were a small detachment. This wasn't by design, but by necessity. The terrain of the Borderlands didn't quite lend itself to platoon-sized battles like the open fields did. No, the fighting for the mine had been close-quarters and brutal. Casualties, whether from blade or fall, had been vast. Surrendering wasn't an option, as there was no love lost between the feuding nations. The age-old tradition of displaying the severed heads of the fallen was alive and well between the men of Tarbent and Bulharo.

Werd and his men were no different. They were warriors of Tarbent, determined to repel the Bulharens from the mountain border. It had been their scouts that had found the treasure buried in the cave. As far as they were concerned, the riches belonged to the great people of Tarbent.

The morning mist obscured their view, not that there was much to see in the mountains. They had been trekking towards the mine for the last few days, eager to wet their blades with Bulharen blood. The only thing his men had wet their swords with was rain.

Werd wrapped his moist cloak around his shoulders and walked up an incline. His armor was chaffing his armpits, and he desperately wanted to unfasten it. The battlefield was no place to become lax, and he knew the moment he loosened his breastplate, a Bulharen arrow would find his flesh.

The men of his small detachment stayed in the gulley. Quickly, their shapes became coated in mist, obscuring them from his view. Sergeant Werd hoped he was heading in the right direction to meet with the scouts.

The three men had been sent out under the cover of darkness, using the moonlight to navigate through the mountains. By midnight, a thick layer of fog had rolled in from the sea. Werd didn't know how much the men could discover, but according to his timepiece, they were due to return.

Sweat and icy rain ran down his chest. The armor had to go, at least for a few minutes. He could hardly see over ten paces in front of him. If the Bulharens had figured out a way to find him in the dense fog, so be it. At least he'd die comfortably. Werd sat on a damp log. There was no sign of the scouts. He hoped they showed up soon. He and his men were eager to get the first fight out of the way. Tales had come of other companies engaged in battle with the enemy, but the only thing they'd fought off was crotch-rot.

Werd removed his helmet and set it next to him. He threw open his cloak and adjusted his belt, pushing his sword out of the way. It wasn't the finest blade around, but a military sword was a utility weapon. Short and stubby, with a leafy-shaped blade, it was good all around, whether it was stabbing or slicing, it would get the job done.

Sergeant Werd fumbled with the leather straps, holding his breastplate snugly to his body. His training and conditioning had gone by the wayside and his waistline was feeling it. Werd's heart was still thumping from the walk up the incline, and he was slick with sweat.

"Yer mother's ass," he whispered to himself. With wet, numb fingers, he loosened the armor. Werd let out a sigh of relief and rubbed the sore spot on his shoulder.

Ahead, in the dense fog, a twig snapped.

"Fuck," he grumbled. He fucking knew it. Fuck the fates.

Werd grabbed the straps, trying to re-tighten them. He stood, not wanting to be caught relaxing by his men. Men who he'd disciplined for less. The breastplate, not fully secured, slid down.

"Dammit," he said. Werd lifted the plate from the bottom and pushed it against his body. The leather buckle caught, and he cinched the armor back over his chest.

Werd threw his helmet on as something moved in the fog.

The scouts had a very distinct whistle that would be sounded in a certain pattern when approaching. Werd, who'd been slightly preoccupied, heard nothing.

His heart was thumping again, never slowing down. This time it wasn't from exertion but from adrenaline. He gripped his sword and took cover behind a tree. If it wasn't his men, but perhaps a Bulharen scout, Werd would ambush them. Hopefully capturing an enemy.

Another sound slowly crept through the fog.

Werd snapped his head towards it in confusion. It was nowhere near the first sound.

Either it was multiple scouts making their way, or it was a man who could walk silently like a specter. He squinted, willing his eyes to cut through the gloom.

There!

Something moved in the fog and this time he could see it. Werd drew steel and hard swallowed. He focused and nearly shrieked when it came into view.

When the cave had been discovered, the surviving scouts were hysterical. They screamed and yelled, claiming the other man had uncovered a monster. An evil beast that had ripped him limb from limb. The only way they could escape was thanks to the sacrifice. They were quickly labeled as cowards and there were whispers of treason, but nothing was done. The amount of wealth they'd described easily made up for the fact they believed in monsters.

Werd had listened as other men talked about the fantastic story, but he took little stock in it. The only thing he knew was that Bulharo had made a move into the Borderlands, and that was unacceptable. When he was a young man, he swore an oath to defend his nation and he would never forget that.

Sergeant Werd watched the four-legged beast stalk through the fog. At that moment, he believed the scouts. Oh, did he believe.

The fog obscured most of the foul beast, but he saw more than enough to know his puny blade would do nothing more than tickle it.

The creature was enormous—slightly bigger than an adult cow. Its head bristled in protrusions, but it didn't look like horns. Instead, they appeared to be stalks. Like him, the beast was wet. Moisture dripped from its belly, as if it had a drooling mouth where its gut should be.

It stopped moving and put its odd face into the air, like a hunting dog. Werd clenched his legs together, praying to hold his piss, which begged to come out. The creature moved on, silently lurching forward toward the decline. Towards his men.

Werd's blade shook. His men were sitting ducks below. They knew not what horror stalked them from the fog above. But what could he do? Yell a warning to them, which would surely turn the beast's ire on him. Attack it, hoping to catch it unaware, slaying it with his steel? Werd did neither, as his decision was made for him.

From the direction the creature had come, came three shrill whistles, followed by a series of others in varying pitches.

Werd gasped. A trickle of urine ran down his leg. He no longer cared as his bladder was released. The scouts had arrived.

The monster stopped. Upon its head, the stalks, which he now knew were topped with hideous eyes, turned back towards the sounds.

Werd clenched the whistle attached to his belt as if it had somehow come to life and blown on its own. He froze, praying the scouts would stay quiet. They did not.

Again, the sequence of whistles blew.

The beast, now with the location of the scouts pinned down, charged into the fog.

He waited a breath and ran, not caring about his footing. The scouts' lives were over, that was certain. Harder Werd sprinted, half sliding down the mountainside. His blade was still clenched tightly in his hand, but he didn't dare pause to sheath it.

And then, the beast found the scouts.

The screams of the doomed men ripped through the air. Werd had heard men die before, and it was never pleasant, but this was something different. The death shrieks were unworldly and hell borne. Werd knew if he didn't warn the rest of his men, they'd all be screaming like that soon.

The wet earth was slick underfoot. Werd did his best not to fall and tumble down the hillside, but it was in vain. Dirt and leaves ran down in front of him like crashing waves. He hopped and jumped over the largest stones, narrowly avoiding breaking his ankle. A root caught his toe and his world rolled.

Werd flipped forward and braced himself. His back struck a rock, knocking the wind from his lungs. He grabbed at anything and everything, trying in vain to slow his descent. The wind rushed by as he fell. Some of his fingernails were reduced to bloody pulp and blackened with grime, but still, he tumbled. Nothing had broken yet, which was a minor miracle. His blade flashed as it tumbled alongside him. Each time, he expected to feel the distinct sting of steel slicing flesh, but he somehow avoided the razor's edge. Another miracle. He only hoped they didn't run out soon. And Werd knew they were going to need a miracle if that beast came for them. His hip smashed into a stunted tree. He bent around it, but finally stopped. Werd was battered and bloody, but on his own two feet again. Only fifty paces away were his men. They all stood and most had swords in hand. A few bowstrings creaked as they were slowly lowered, and the tension released.

"Sergeant Werd, are you okay?" Corporal Saloly asked. The corporal rushed forward, sheathing his sword, and he helped his commanding officer down the rest of the hill.

Werd was out of breath and in pain, but he spoke. He sheathed his sword. "A beast." He pointed to the area he'd just come from. "A fucking demon on four legs. In the fog." He slowed to catch his breath. "The fucking scouts. It's fucking killing them." Werd spat. Blood and dirt flew from his mouth. He wiped the gore from his eyes. During his fall, his forehead took a hit, splitting wide open. His dirty fingers smeared the redness over his skin like savage war paint.

The men looked up into the fog but could see nothing. Each of their heads snapped around, as if something would snatch them from the gray.

"A monster?" Saloly asked. He wasn't one to question authority, but even coming from a no-nonsense man like Werd, it sounded far-fetched.

"Fuck yes. The scouts, the ones they called crazy and traitors, weren't lying."

A rock tumbled down the hillside, bouncing along the way. The men heard it falling, trying to pick it up in the fog. It bounced hard and landed in their midst. Except it wasn't a rock. It was the head of one scout—the whistle still clenched between his teeth.

Saloly released Werd, letting the Sergeant fall to the ground. "To arms!" he yelled, again drawing steel.

The rest of the men didn't need an order, and almost all of them already had their blades in hand. Each of them looked up towards the fog.

The beast moved, sending more debris toward the soldiers.

"Oh, fuck," one of them muttered.

Werd turned just in time to see the creature descend on his man.

It wasn't graceful, like the pounce of a hunting cat, but an attack of sheer violence. The beast leaped from the hillside, ignoring the sword in the soldier's hand. A clawed foot entered flesh and drove Werd's man to the ground. The impact against the mountain floor was wet, but still with the sound of crunching bones. Another of the monster's hellish appendages joined in and began ripping at the dead man. A mouth bristling with long fangs opened underneath the monster's body. Where a normal animal would have a belly, it had a gaping maw. The soldier's flesh ripped apart in wet red and blue, as his entrails were torn free. With a chunk of man-meat clenched in a claw, the beast fed. Blood dripped from its mouth as it crammed more and more of the soldier into it.

"Kill it, you fucking cowards!" Werd found his voice and screamed. "Kill it!" His commands were given, but he didn't move closer to the monster.

Arrows struck its mud-colored hide, bouncing from it like it was steel.

Saloly, noticing the men stood frozen and Sergeant Werd wasn't rushing in to kill the beast, raised his sword and moved in. "On me!" Saloly rushed to the right flank of the beast. The eyes of the creature were dancing around like it had a host of snakes on its head. Saloly didn't look behind him, but heard the shuffling of boots at his rear. He knew he wasn't alone.

Some men were veterans, moving with caution alongside Saloly. The smell of human entrails and the rest of the mutilated corpse caused some of them to slow. Not Saloly. He knew this thing needed to be killed and killed quickly. If not, it would decimate their ranks. Death needed to be swift, so as not to waste the life of their man, who'd become a meal for the monster.

Two spearmen flanked the creature from the opposite side. Stalk-eyes followed them, but the

45

monster didn't stop in its feeding. Even when the spears stabbed out, the creature didn't flinch.

Saloly was just about in sword range, but was watching the attack from the other side. He knew the monster could see the spearmen, but it was far from concerned. Over his years, he'd hunted many animals, including boar. His father had used hunting dogs, having them hold the wild animal with their powerful jaws while the killing blow was delivered with a specialized spear. Even then, the boar would have a primal understanding of what the spear was. It knew, deep down, it was about to die. At the last moment, it would flinch, but not be able to turn away from the steel. This creature in front of them was dumb or unafraid. Saloly hoped for the prior.

The spears hit the monster's flank with a thrust that would've impaled two men... and shattered them. Steel blades bent and the shafts erupted into splinters. The spearmen's momentum carried them forward; each with a shocked look on their faces.

With its right claw, the beast attacked, going low. Its powerful appendage struck the first man mid-thigh, snapping his left leg. His jagged femur burst from his uniform, impaling his right inner thigh. He fell to the ground screaming and twisted.

The second spearman tripped over his comrade, falling face-first onto the ground. He scurried, trying desperately to get back to his feet. Wet leaves and dirt slid, making traction almost impossible.

The monster raised its foot and stomped, crushing the soldier's head. Like a rotten melon falling from a roof, the sound of his bursting skull echoed against the rocks.

Saloly was too close to retreat. His only option was to attack, even though he knew it was futile. He gripped his sword in both hands and raised it above his head. If he was going to kill this beast, it wouldn't be from slashes. No, he needed to stab it and stab it deep. He just hoped it had a heart to sever. Stalks of eyes were following him, and his other men, watching the incoming attack. The beast turned as his blade struck.

Saloly braced himself, praying he'd feel the telltale sign of his sword entering flesh. With a primal grunt, he stabbed.

The sword snapped as if hitting a brick wall. Around him, the rest of the blades bounced harmlessly from the hide of the monster.

Saloly would never die easily, that was for certain. He dropped the shattered remains of his sword and drew his belt knife. A man next to him renewed his attack with another fearful chop into the seemingly indestructible hide of the creature.

With its focus firmly on them, the creature turned and struck. It reared up on its hind legs, like a circus bear. The mouth on its belly bristled with teeth. Wedged firmly in between some of them were the remnants of their former man-in-arms.

Saloly dodged the first swipe, narrowly missing a decapitating blow as the claws swung overhead. The man next to him wasn't as lucky.

He tried to duck but was far too late. His head was turned sideways as the beast's leg impacted his skull. A rent of flesh and blood opened as the killing blow partially decapitated the soldier.

Saloly was more vulnerable than he'd ever felt. His knife was useless in the face of such a beast. Knowing he had no other option, he threw the blade at the creature's mouth and turned to run.

Sergeant Werd and the rest of the men who'd thought better than to engage the creature watched. Saloly saw the looks of fear on their faces, and he braced himself.

A pressure, unlike anything Saloly had ever felt, crushed his midsection. He was weightless, like a feather on the breeze. Around his waist was wrapped the monster's claw. Gnarled, filthy talons were burrowed into his flesh, but they didn't hurt at the moment. What did was the pressure, the lack of air, and the burning deep in his gut. Saloly was ripped from his feet and yanked backward. He snapped his head around at the last second and saw nothing but teeth.

CHAPTER 7

It had been a week since Sorrow and Jagrim had set out, looking for female companionship. Ayr was a city known for its women, but it seemed like all the whores had gone underground. Many of them had taken to inns and apartments, doing business in a strict manner. Most of them hired thugs for protection and to shakedown any prospective clientele. This came with a price, raising the fee of even the lowliest of prostitutes. Having to deal with a thug and getting patted down wasn't the most attractive thing to men. There was no way Sorrow would surrender his blade to some tough-turned-pimp, especially knowing the Church could be looking for him. It was a quick way to find himself in chains again, and soon after, at the end of a rope. Or worse, crucified in the city square of Vartacian.

Sorrow sat at a table with an untouched plate of food in front of him. His beer was going flat, but the pipe he'd been puffing on was burning strong. The sweet smell of tobac mingled with the scent of food in the tavern. Some men huddled around the small table, gnawing away at their plates.

The tavern was full of men. There were no jovial conversations coming from any of them. A dour mood fell over the men of Ayr, with the price of pussy being driven up far too much for the working man. Still, more and more men poured into the city on boats, jumping off with a gleam in their eyes. That gleam was dulled before they even left the docks. Veterans of Ayr expected to be greeted by willing whores at the docks, albeit not the best of women, but still something warm and wet. When they'd only seen other frustrated men lurking about, they knew something had changed.

With them came frustration and violence, but men carried something else: information.

The battle at the Borderlands was heating up, and both sides were taking casualties. The demand for fighting men was at an all-time high, even though the fighting had just started.

From the first time Jagrim had mentioned the conflict, Sorrow wasn't much interested. But the prospect of collecting heads, now that was a much better offer. If he could get paid just as much to cut heads from the dead and not have to worry about getting killed, he was fine with that. That was the very reason that had brought them to the tavern.

"So, what are we doing here, Sorrow?" asked Zakkas. The dark-skinned man leaned back in his chair. He had a mug of watered-down wine and bread in front of him. After spending the better part of his time with his people, the commoner food disgusted him. His scalp was scraped clean and his eyes shone in the lantern light.

"I feel like it's time we pulled up anchor and left Ayr. The work here is meager and the entire city feels like it's wound to bursting." As if to accent his point, a quick fight broke out near the bar. Fists flew and drinks were spilled, but bystanders restrained the combatants, pushing them into the street before more men joined in. Violence was contagious and once it started going, there was no stopping it. Sorrow nodded, but didn't speak. "I, like many of you, are not suited for dock work. The smell of fish disgusts me, and I have no interest in being a pimp. Those, it seems, are the two most prevalent jobs left in this city."

Nods came from the other men, well, most of them. Fin just stared, taking it in.

Sorrow sipped at this beer, catching the gaze of the youngest in the bunch. He put the mug down and wiped his mouth. "Our ship, courtesy of the Church, has been re-outfitted. Jagrim and I have sold off most of the Church items and will split the bounty with all the remaining crew."

"Most of the bounty, I'm sure," barked Gortul. The wide man sucked something out of his teeth.

"We did the legwork," said Jagrim, cutting Sorrow off. "If your fat ass wanted to walk around all of Ayr, hawking stolen material, you should've let us know."

Gortul picked at a piece of hard cheese on his plate, his eyes down. "I'm just saying," he grumbled.

Sorrow looked at them, seeing if anyone else

had a problem with the distribution of the funds. None spoke. "Now, the question is, where do we go?"

Fin looked around at the other men. "Why do we have to leave? The whores can't stay tucked away forever, and there are plenty of other jobs. We might have to move into another district." He rubbed his chin. "Maybe the textile district would have more for us. And I'm sure the women there would be more than willing to wet our cocks."

"We're not talking about whores, Fin. I was talking about becoming a pimp. Something I don't want any part of. Yes, the reluctance of the whores has made things less than enjoyable, but who knows how far this dry spell stretches? What if we move further inland and find it the same? Whores in hiding, only hiring the roughest men to guard them. No, that isn't something I want. But feel free to venture out on your own. You'll be given your funds to do with what you want."

Fin looked at Sorrow as he spoke, but his eyes drifted past the man. It was only for a second, but Sorrow felt it; someone was watching him.

"Besides, moving further inland isn't my first choice, especially with the vessel we sailed in on."

"And why is that?" asked Gortul.

"The Church of the Refining Light. One of their largest churches is just outside the textile district. It's doubtful word has reached them about Vicar Prentas, but there is no reason to lurk closer to them. Eventually, they'll find out and send their men after us," Sorrow said.

Each man nodded, as if they'd forgotten about the bloody battle they'd been in only weeks in the past.

Fin's eyes snapped past Sorrow again with a glimmer of recognition. This time, he pushed his chair back from the table.

Sorrow turned his head, following Fin's eyes.

Three men were making their way over. They stumbled and stunk of alcohol and urine, but had blades at their waist. With a bottle in hand, the lead man stopped in front of Sorrow. He was fat, and greasy, stinking to hell and back. His shirt was stretched tight over his belly and he eyed Fin.

"I thought it was you, you little cunt," the fat man said. He put the bottle to his lips and drank.

Fin had a shocked look on his face, but Sorrow could sniff out a lie from across the room. Regardless of what the boy was about to utter, he knew this man.

"Who, me?" Fin asked.

"Yeah, you. You stole my girl and my fucking knife." The fat man dropped the empty bottle on the floor. It didn't shatter and rolled away on the unevenness of the wooden planks. His hand went to a short sword at his belt. "Now give it back, or I'll cut yer little cock off and take it."

Sorrow, being the closest to the three, pushed his chair back and stood. "Now, friend, I think you're mistaken." He pointed towards Fin, but kept his eyes on the men. Jagrim and the others rose as well, but no one had drawn steel. Yet.

The rest of the tavern had grown quiet. Their bloodlust was still up from the previous fight, and some grumbled it was stopped too early. The looks and chatter coming from the crowd seemed as if they were ready for another one. A fistfight was good, but a fight with blades was even better. This time, no one moved to intervene.

"I might be a fucking drunk, but my eyes and my cock work just fine," the fat man grumbled. His companions were sizing up the other men, but hadn't drawn their weapons either. "And I know it was you. The other night. You took my whore and my blade. The whore I don't care about, but that fucking knife was pure silver. And I plan on getting it back."

Fin pulled his cloak back slightly, showing his sword and the knife. "I was wondering why it was so heavy," he said with a smirk. There was no point in arguing with the man any longer, especially with the knife on him. Fin drew his sword a few inches from the sheath, letting the blade shimmer in the lantern light. "I'll gladly meet you in the alley, if you'd like a chance to get your knife back."

The fat man stared at him. His beady eyes were glassy, but seemed to still contain a glimpse of common sense. The size difference was vast, with him being larger by many pounds, but steel didn't care about weight. Now he was in a spot he didn't think he'd be in. A younger, smaller man had called him out. The room was silent, watching the exchange.

The fat man hocked back and spat on the floor. "Out back, ya little cunt."

A cheer rose among the patrons and chairs slid as they stood.

Fin smiled and pushed his sword back into the sheath.

"Looks like we might leave sooner than we expected," Jagrim said to Sorrow. The fat man had no chance of beating Fin, that they knew.

"Looks that way," Sorrow said, following the crowd out into the street. A boy was walking by with a sack over his shoulder. The burlap was wet and dripping, with the stink of fish wafting from it. "Boy," Sorrow yelled, trying to keep up with the crowd as they rounded the corner towards the back of the tavern. The young fishmonger stopped and was on high alert. When no threat was presented, he softened just slightly. "A fishmonger?" Sorrow asked, pointing to the sack on the boy's back.

"Yes, sir. Me father and I are fishermen. 'Tis an old catch gone rotten. Bringing it back for the morrow's bait."

Sorrow dug into his purse, opposite his blade. He pulled a handful of coppers from the leather pouch. "Did ye see the old Church ship in the harbor?"

The boy picked a scale from his shirt and flicked it. "Aye, I did. I saw a Church ship, but no Church folk on board. Some men are still on the ship, sir."

Sorrow handed him the coppers and took the

sack from his shoulder. "Here, this is for your catch, and then some." He tossed the stinking bag on the ground. "Now, run to that ship and tell the men onboard that we'll be leaving tonight. You hear me?"

The boy nodded. A few feral cats, scarred and battered, sniffed at the rotting fish.

"You see this?" Sorrow held up his hand, showing off his tattoo. "Tell them the man with the snake on his hand sent you."

Without another word, the boy ran. His stench helped clear the way.

A shout arose from behind the building. Sorrow worked his way through the alley and saw the crude circle of men surrounding Fin and the fat man. Bets were running wild through the crowd, but the fighting hadn't started. A few men had taken lanterns from inside the tavern, using them to cast a warm glow in the dark alley.

Sorrow pushed through to find Jagrim.

Jagrim stroked his red beard with one hand but kept the other hand on his axe. In the center of the circle were Fin and the fat man, but others were eyeing them as well. And it wasn't only the two men who'd confronted them in the tavern.

Sorrow noticed it, too. Sets of eyes, eyes belonging to hard men, watched their small group. He didn't know if they were agents of the Church, bounty hunters, or just men looking to kill. Either way, they'd been noticed by Sorrow.

Good, let them stare. They are nothing to us. Let us do what we do best: kill. They are cunts, the lot of them. Pull your blade, Sorrow. Shed their blood and wet the earth. Make their loved ones lament and weep as we've done so many times before.

Sorrow flexed his tattooed hand, willing his mind to quiet. He had to admit, the feeling of steel parting living flesh was unlike anything else he'd experienced. It was a close second only to his cock entering a woman—something he hadn't had in a while.

"I sent a boy to ready the ship," Sorrow said. He followed Jagrim's gaze to the men staring them down.

"Aye, good idea. I have a feeling we've overstayed our welcome in Ayr." Jagrim shifted his weight as if an attack was coming. A man, one with a puckered scar on his cheek, spat, but never broke eye contact. "We might have to fight our way back to the ship."

Yes! Kill them all!

"Wouldn't be my first time," Sorrow said.

"Hey, be careful!" the scarred man in the crowd yelled. The fat man looked sick, like he didn't want to be there any longer. Knife be damned. His face was green, and he was about to puke. Still, he turned to the man, yelling. "This lot of cunts are with the Church. A group of sick fucks, all of them." A grumble went up amongst the crowd and more eyes snapped towards Fin. "Them, and him," the man said. He pointed at Sorrow and the rest of the crew.

"Aye, we saw yer ship in the port. The worst

kind of sell-swords, cunts that work for the blasted fucks of Refining Light," the new man said, spitting on the ground.

Sorrow felt the tension growing around them. Over the weeks, it had been harder and harder to find buyers for the Church property. No one knew what to make of it. It wasn't every day that someone sold off Church wares and word had spread. Politics wasn't his game, never was, but he wished he knew a bit more about the city they were in.

"I heard the Church was raising the dead," another man said.

"Aye, they are digging up the bones of the dead for their sickening rituals," another yelled.

"Fucking pimps and kid fuckers, the lot of them."

The fat man could feel the crowd swaying away from the fight, something he seemed grateful for. "Aye, this little fucker is a thief, too." And then a revelation snapped into his alcohol-soaked head. "I bet he's the one killing the whores." The crowd gasped. "No wonder we can't get no pussy. This motherfucker is scaring away our women."

"This is going to get ugly," Sorrow said. His hand was on his blade, ready to draw.

"Aye," Jagrim said. Zakkas and Gortul stood next to him, each of them ready to burst into action.

Fin stared at the fat man and slowly drew his steel. "Enough stalling, you sack of fat. Draw your blade or I'll cut you down where you stand."

The fat man, sensing the crowd on his side,

laughed. "The fight is not just with me, you little cur. It is you, isn't it? You're the limp-dick killing the whores. Yer the reason we can't get our dicks wet. Yer the reas--," his words were cut off as Fin's sword entered just under his belly button.

Fin pulled it out quickly, taking a lump of yellow fat with the blade.

The fat man was quiet, looking down at the new hole in his body. His chubby hands touched the gore running from his gut in disbelief.

Fin wasn't done. He thrust again, this time aiming higher. The honed edge of his blade cracked ribs and pierced the heart of the fat man. Again, he yanked his blade from the man's body, this time ushering forth more blood.

The fat man fell to his knees in front of the now-silent crowd. His hands, more accustomed to grabbing food and unwilling flesh, now tried to contain arterial blood as it coursed down his disgusting shirt.

Fin, knowing his man was defeated, spun his sword with a flourish. He looked at the crowd, almost willing someone new to step forward. The hunger in his eyes craved death. It was a look Sorrow knew all too well.

"Murder. Yer a fucking murderer," the scarred man said. He looked up from the now-dead man, who was face down in the alley. At first, he hesitated to draw steel, but saw men next to him pulling their blades.

Fin looked at them. "Come on! I'll fucking gut

the lot of ye!"

"Should we get him?" Gortul asked. His mace was in his hand, but kept low and out of sight.

"Aye, we might have to," Jagrim said, drawing his axe.

"Fucking pink skins," Zakkas muttered, but still drew his wicked curved sword.

The four of them pushed through the crowd toward their shipmate, weapons at the ready.

"The City Watch!" someone yelled from the mouth of the alley.

The crowd grew frantic as the shrill sound of whistles cut through the night air.

Sorrow and his men looked around as everyone sheathed their weapons and ran.

A cluster of armored men wielding cudgels descended on the impromptu crowd. No orders were given, just beatings, as men tried to avoid the heavy clubs. The dull thud of ironwood on flesh was heard, along with the rush of air being kicked out of lungs.

"I think it's time to go," Jagrim said. He put his axe on his belt and dodged a watchman's club as it came towards his head. He tripped the man, pushing him hard to the ground.

The rest of them secured their weapons and entered the melee, hoping to escape to the ship without a cracked skull.

CHAPTER 8

One month later

Sorrow stood at the bow of the stolen ship as it was guided into the harbor. The emblem of the Church of the Refining Light had been removed from the mast. Since Sorrow had partially decapitated Vicar Prentas and murdered his acolyte, Brother Kirsh, he didn't think it was proper to fly that flag any longer. Not to mention he hated the fucking Church. A new flag, one painted out of boredom by his companion, Jagrim, flew instead of the sun emblem of the Church.

The flag, a tattered piece of sailcloth bearing a black snake, snapped in the breeze. The snake wasn't a perfect replica of the one tattooed on Sorrow's right hand, but it was close enough. Jagrim never claimed to be an artist, at least with paint. With his axe...now that was another story.

The ship, which they'd declined to name, was pulled against a dock. Thick ropes were tossed overboard and gnarled dock hands fastened them to wooden posts. Albeit with a steady slew of curses, the knots were tight.

Sorrow watched the dock workers scrambling around, moving from one ship to another. War was great for commerce, that was for sure. Ships of all shapes and sizes floated in the disgusting water. Flotsam, seaweed, and a thin sheen of rainbow-slicked oil bobbed in the murkiness. Men and women crowded the docks, all trying to cut out a small fortune from the blood and sweat of others. Sorrow and his men were there for the same reason.

The world ran on blood and money, and no matter what anyone said, it was always better to have money. If you could keep your blood and not spill anyone else's, even better. But, as Sorrow and his men knew, murder and money went hand-in-hand.

Bloodshed was something very common in the stretch of mountains known only as the Borderlands.

The Borderlands were a barren and mostly uninhabitable mountain range separating the nations of Tarbent and Bulharo. It was craggy and littered with thick patches of scrub brush and stunted trees. There wasn't much to it and neither nation cared to stake claim to it. That was, until a group of scouts stumbled across a deep cave.

A vein of ore and gems like nothing ever seen before was unearthed in that cave. Unburied, and pulled into the light. The scouts, the living ones, told their leaders about the cave. Their babble was almost incoherent, speaking about a creature in the darkness. At some point, they'd said the magic words: gold and gems. That was it. No one cared or even thought of whatever scared the men. Greed was the only thing on their minds. Many men wrote the scouts' story off as nonsense. They were victims of the elements, and their brains had suffered from it. Monsters were things in children's tales, not in the real world.

Before long, Bulharo's spies, many of whom were deeply embedded in Tarbent society, caught wind of this newly discovered mine. Considering it was in the Borderlands, it was fair game. Before long, miners from both nations set out, hoping to find this cave, which the scouts refused to even look for again. Miners ended up dead, and soon they were accompanied by soldiers. Both nations sent men, some with shovels and some with swords, into those mountains. Miners from Tarbent had been the first to find the cave and quickly began mining the riches.

The gangplank was set against the side of their ship. Sorrow put a boot on the wooden ramp and adjusted his sword belt.

He still hadn't replaced the length of cheap steel. It had served him well and still held quite an edge. In Ayr, he thought about upgrading but declined. A man could be killed with a sharp piece of wood. There was no need to spend his pilfered fortune on a fancy blade. He'd save that money for sins of flesh and alcohol. The good stuff, not the swill Jagrim drank. The sword would do and had yet to fail him. The tip was pointy and the edges sharp; what more could a man ask for?

The gangplank swayed with the bobbing ship, but Sorrow's sea legs seemed like permanent fixtures. He started down the ramp, eager to get on dry land and have a hot meal. Maybe even enjoy some warm flesh, too. After the lack of women he'd experienced in Ayr, he could use a good fuck. He knew his men were behind him; he never looked back.

"Aye, do you have your little knife?" Jagrim asked Finleos, who was walking ahead of him down the ramp.

Fin didn't turn to look at the older man with the wild red beard. "Yes, I have my knife. My knife that I'll be able to sell for triple what it's worth."

Jagrim let out a belly laugh, but it wasn't him that responded to the young man's statement. It was barrel-chested Gortul.

"Yes, all noble warriors need an apple peeler made of silver. Especially one that got us run out of one of the best cities this side of the world. Ya had to swipe it from that fat slob, didn't ye?"

Fin stepped onto the wooden dock and turned. "Oh, and don't forget that I killed him in front of his cocksucking friends." Absently, he touched the knife on his belt.

As if any of them could forget that indiscretion. Fin's nimble fingers and fast blade had landed them in trouble. Not to mention the accusations the fat man threw at him about killing the whores. He may have been the reason the pussy had dried up so abruptly and was coming at a premium price.

The knife wasn't flashy, but he knew it was worth money, especially in a war-torn area. The fat man yelled about it being silver, and Fin knew it to be true. He only wondered where the man had stolen it from in the first place. There was no way he bought such an expensive knife. Not when his clothes were in such disrepair and hygiene left something to be desired. The blade was damn near pure. This wasn't an instrument of war, no, but it could be sold or melted down for money, which could buy actual weapons. Not only did he have his earnings from the Church's loot they'd stolen from the ship, but he had the knife.

"Aye, leave the lad alone. It sure made for an interesting night, I'll say that. Maybe next time, buy some whores instead of stealing, okay?" Jagrim smirked. "Or maybe you didn't need whores. Yer quite handsome. Wouldn't you say, Sorrow? I mean, he looks like you and you still needed to pay for a fuck, so maybe I'm wrong." Jagrim laughed and clapped Sorrow on the shoulder.

Gortul stood with them. "Eh, maybe Finny doesn't *like* the fairer sex." He bumped his shoulder into Fin. "Could ye want to stick your prick in a nice, hairy arse?"

Fin knew they were fooling, but it still grated on him. If only they saw the women he *was* with in Ayr. The women with slit throats and scared looks in their eyes. Now that was something money couldn't buy.

"Gortul, I wouldn't fuck your stumpy arse if it was the last arse in the world. That's for sure."

Zakkas walked down the gangplank as nimble as a cat. "What's this talk about arse fucking? You pink-skins have some strange traditions."

Sorrow tuned them out as best as he could. They were late. The battle for the mine had been going on for months, at least according to the traders in Ayr. It wasn't too late for them to capitalize on others' misfortune, but they couldn't waste time.

The dock was a floating street filled with stinking humans. Inland, and off the dock, was a small fishing village. Even from his vantage point, Sorrow knew the chances of finding a room or a meal were for naught.

"We march," Sorrow said, looking back at the group of men. Some of the original mercenaries had gotten off the ship at Ayr and stayed, not rejoining them. But a few, more like a handful, stayed loyal. They were almost drawn to Sorrow. To his charisma and guile. Not to mention, his use of blood magic had made him a legend. Little did they know, he didn't have any spells or tricks left up his sleeve. Just steel, a quick hand, and no mercy.

"And where to?" Jagrim stood next to him, looking over the crowd. A buxom prostitute walked in front of them and wiggled her hips. "I mean, we have time for one night in the town, right?"

Sorrow watched the woman. As much as he'd enjoy a quick fuck, time was of the essence. One look at the rough men and women, and he knew they weren't the only ones there to profit from war and heads.

"I don't think so," Sorrow said, much to the disappointment of his friend.

Jagrim looked defeated.

"But when we cash in, you'll have plenty of money to waste on loose women and gut rot."

That brought a smile to Jagrim's face. "Aye, let's get moving then." He started walking, parting the crowd with his body and a flurry of profanity.

CHAPTER 9

Sergeant Rugan looked at the few men he had with him. They were veterans, most of them, but a few young men had been tasked to his small squad. Each man carried a crossbow and a short sword. Trigger fingers itched, but the men held. They waited, their ambush ready, hoping to get the chance to bury a bolt in the enemy. To watch them die before them, their blood wetting the rocks of the Borderland. To feel the edge of their blades hack through flesh and bone to remove their heads. A grisly trophy, but a warning for those that would fight against Tarbent.

The ambush had been set for the better part of the day. The choke point Sergeant Rugan and his men were positioned above was a natural funnel. Any advancing men from Bulharo would have to cross their path or take a much longer route. The mine, which was no longer considered a cave now that ore was being moved, was behind them. After it was confirmed, operations to extract the riches began immediately. Soon after, blood was being shed. Small fights here and there, with only squad-sized groups killing each other. Killing and decapitating.

Rugan didn't know when or how the grisly tradition had started, but he knew it was alive and well. The two nations, which were said to have been formed by two brothers, had always displayed the heads of their enemies. It was barbaric, and he didn't enjoy having to carry the extra weight back, but it was part of their assignment. As long as his head stayed where it was, he didn't mind. He'd cut off a few Bulharo heads and be done with it.

Corporal Sager looked at Sergeant Rugan. Sager was positioned to Rugan's left. He and three men were behind a boulder, but shielded by a small copse of trees. They had the best vantage point and could see quite a way. Sager pointed at his eyes and made a series of hand motions.

Rugan nodded and relayed the message to a young private. "Ten men, from the east. Staggered groups of three, three, and four. Light armor, spears, and swords. Quietly, spread the word. Corporal Sager and his men will fire the first volley; do not fire until they do."

The private, who wasn't even able to shave yet, nodded. His eyes were wide. This, Rugan knew, was the boy's first taste of combat. He wasn't expecting much of a fight. That was the point of an ambush, wasn't it? Put crossbow bolts into your enemy, finish the wounded with blades, and take their heads. Shouldn't take more than minutes, if that.

The private quickly and gently made his way to the other small groups of men. Sergeant Rugan watched and received nods from all of them. The private came back just as quietly as he'd gone out. Rugan was impressed, but didn't say so. He didn't want the boy to get an ego before his first fight.

"Here," Rugan handed the private a crossbow. "Aim for the chest and make your shot count."

The private took the bow and squeezed it tight. His grip made the wood and leather of the weapon creak.

"Steady," Sergeant Rugan said. "Just relax, aim, and squeeze. This will be all over soon."

The private swallowed and nodded, but still looked like he had a frog in his throat.

Rugan looked at Corporal Sager, who was aiming, along with the men he had with him.

"Carefully peek out and pick out a man. Don't look at his face, just focus on his belly and squeeze."

The private closed his eyes for a moment, licked his lips, and moved to the side of the outcropping he shared with the Sergeant. In the distance, which wasn't too far, a man walked into view. The private used the crude sight and stuck it on the man's belly. He kept one eye closed and tried to steady his racing heart. The blood rushed through his ears, sounding like the surf, but he did his best to keep still. Once the first shot was fired, he would shoot. It seemed like an eternity, but he held his aim.

The *twang* of a bowstring echoed through the air and was immediately followed up by screaming.

More bows released, sending short crossbow bolts into the unsuspecting men. The private's finger hovered over the trigger and the man's face came into view.

He wasn't much older than him, if at all, and was scared. The young soldier was looking around as his fellow men were cut down. His hand shook; his spear dancing in his grip.

The private closed his eyes and fired. The bolt didn't make it to the man's belly, but caught him right below the left eye. Gray fletching from the bolt stuck from the man's face. His mouth opened and locked in place, like a dead fish. He fell face-first, dead, onto the stony ground. The tip of the bolt burst from the back of his skull, glistening red in the sunlight.

"Well done, boy," Sergeant Rugan said. He held his crossbow. It too was empty, his bolt finding flesh. "See, over in seconds." He scanned the area. The Bulharo men were down. Most of them were dead, but some still moaned in pain. They'd be dead soon. "Now," he said, drawing his sword, "let's collect some fucking heads." Sergeant Rugan left his cover, the other men following his lead.

Injured men begged for mercy, seeing the Tarbent soldiers coming towards them with the gleam of murder in their eyes.

"I'll give ya mercy, ya fucking cunts!" Sergeant Rugan growled. He'd reached the first wounded man.

"Mercy," the man begged, holding a bloody

hand towards Sergeant Rugan.

"Here's some mercy, you Bulharo fuck," Rugan raised his sword above his head, preparing to stab the man. Something hit him in the stomach and suddenly, he couldn't breathe. He looked down and saw an arrow poking from his shirt. It was deep, embedded halfway into his body. Something fell next to him. The private, the young boy who was so full of life, lay dead. An arrow sprouted from his throat. The boy's lifeblood wet the stones. The stones where they'd all die.

Rugan dropped his sword and fell to his knees. His men around him turned and looked into the trees. Arrows flew and screams rose.

The Bulharo men, the primary force hidden behind the decoy, rushed forward. Their blades shimmered and their smiles were wide. Blood splashed on the stones and trees.

Rugan watched the battle, waiting for a blade to find him. He knew, before the night was over, his head would be gone.

CHAPTER 10

The battlefield wasn't much of a hike through the mountains. Fighting was going on all over the Borderlands, with small skirmishes popping up everywhere. Sorrow and his men hiked, passing other mercenaries along the way. They never came to blows, but more than one standoff happened in the crags of the Borderlands. All of them were there for the same reason: money. But every other merc making their way into the mountains was just another fighter that could steal from their bounty.

Death was everywhere, but the corpses were all freshly decapitated. Some of them were so mangled and rotten, they'd bypassed them altogether. The small group of men moved further, deeper into the mountains. Sorrow was second-guessing his decision to venture into the war-torn nation. If they didn't make any money, or lost a man to injury, it would be a failure.

On the voyage over, the ship had nearly succumbed to mutiny. Some of the remaining men, those that had stayed aboard, didn't agree with the destination. It was rumored that Fin had riled them up, but no one would admit that. Some of them asked to reroute to Graathull, which Sorrow didn't think was a bad idea. But he knew the Church money would only take them so far. If they could increase their purse with a few heads and bounties, the better. So, they stayed the course to the Borderlands. One man, Jasen, made the mistake of drawing steel against Sorrow. Apparently, Jasen had been a bit more dedicated to the Church than the others. Gortul, without a word, broke Jasen's arm and threw him overboard. That quickly ended any thought of mutiny.

They'd just finished a mid-day meal of bread and dried meat when they heard it.

A battle, and a violent one at that.

Sorrow and his men listened. There was fighting going on, that was for sure. It sounded intense and bloody; the best kind of fighting always was. Screams and curses echoed through the mountains, but within moments, all sound ceased. At least the sound of steel on steel. Low moaning and cries of anguish could be heard on the wind.

"Sounds like a good time," Jagrim said. "Probably an ambush." His axe was in hand, but there was no one to swing it at. Still, the bigger warrior held it at the ready. He hadn't made it as long as he had by being stupid and unprepared.

"Yeah, a real fucking blast," Gortul said. His mace was still on his belt, but his hand rested on it, ready to draw the weapon.

Sorrow looked up at the sun and nodded.

"Let's give it an hour or two. Let the wounded die and survivors leave. Then we can collect our heads and cash in." The men with him nodded. There weren't many of them left after leaving Ayr, but a few stuck around. In the Borderlands, it was better to travel with a smaller bunch, as opposed to a full squad of men. If they'd been at the same amount as they were fighting the necromancer, they would've had issues.

"How about we just go up now and ambush the survivors?" Fin asked. His sword was drawn, and he was using it to point toward the sound of dying men. "We can jump them, kill them all, and get even more heads." A gleam shone in his eye, similar to that of when he killed the fat man in Ayr.

The sound of more steel on steel rang out through the mountains. Screams rose and fell. Grunts echoed and cries stirred between the trees and rocks.

"Fuckers," Jagrim muttered. "A counter-ambush." He crouched as if a crossbow bolt was heading for him. He scanned the crags, but there was nothing to see, only hear.

Jagrim looked at the young man. "See, that's why we don't rush in." He pointed towards the melee. "Boy, the best fight is the one that never happens. I, for one, don't want steel shoved into my guts. I'm not sure about you, but I can do without that."

"Agreed," Zakkas said. His curved sword was sheathed, but like Gortul, his hand rested on the pommel. "We wait, like Sorrow said, and then go. Let them finish killing each other and collect. A large enough fight can land us with a good payday. I doubt they'll even take every head, if any. A good leader will treat his wounded before concerning himself with trophies of war. At least, I hope, for our purses' sake."

Jagrim, realizing the battle wasn't coming to them, stood and walked over to Fin. His axe hung from his hand and he patted Fin on the shoulder. "I know you have a bloodlust, Fin, but don't worry, you have plenty of years to wet yer blade. But this isn't that kind of day. This is a day of easy money and get the fuck off this blasted rock." Jagrim secured his axe, allowing it to hang from his belt.

Fin looked at him and nodded. An urge washed over him, an urge to shove his blade into Jagrim's gut, but he didn't. He spun his sword with a flourish and slid his blade back into the sheath. Fin smirked at Jagrim, doing his best to hold the fake smile. It wavered and never touched his eyes.

Sorrow stared at the young man. That harsh coldness in Fin's glare glinted like hard steel. He'd seen it when he first laid eyes on the boy when they'd met on the beach months earlier. It was cold and uncaring, and he'd seen it before...in a mirror. That stare could've belonged to him when he was in the Kresh'i fighting pits. A lust for death, whether the enemy or his own, was always there. Sorrow couldn't wait for his next fight to spill blood in front of a roaring crowd. His sword was always for sale, trying to repay the mental debt he'd gathered over the years.

"We'd might as well settle in and let them die. Hopefully, the victors head the opposite way, but if not, set up a perimeter," Sorrow said.

They spread out in silence, ensuring they didn't become the next victims of an ambush. It wasn't the first time most of them had fought in a strange land, but none of them wanted it to be their last. On the wind, they listened, hoping the moans of the dying men would cease. They didn't. In the mountains, men died and died horribly.

Hours had passed and Sorrow swallowed a mouthful of wine; the last bit he had left. He looked up at the sun, which was getting lower. "Come on," he said, as he stood. "We need to get up there and see what we're dealing with." The sounds from the battlefield ahead had quieted. Whoever had won either went the other direction, or lay dying with the losers. Either way, Sorrow didn't want to wait any longer to find out.

The mountain was rough in some spots, leaving men to climb massive boulders and short cliffs. Other sections resembled a rocky and sparse forest. It was unpredictable and Sorrow was glad it wasn't his men doing the fighting on those bluffs.

It didn't take long for them to find the battleground. Carrion birds were already circling the dead, and some would dip down to claim a meal.

Sorrow thought back to the beach where he'd washed up only months earlier. The gulls had made a feast of his bloated and dead shipmates. He drew his sword and heard steel leaving leather around him.

The small battleground was littered with bodies. Some were filled with arrows or crossbow bolts; others were mercilessly hacked apart. Coagulated blood and glistening offal decorated the floor. The entire area smelled of spilled innards and shit. Black birds, some with wet, red beaks, danced away as the men approached. They cawed and flew into the trees, waiting for their time to return, watching the men with beady eyes.

The dead were everywhere, but there were survivors, too. Men groaned but writhed little. Instead, they saved their energy by trying to hold in lifeblood and slit bellies.

Sorrow looked around and began counting. Almost every man still had their head, which meant this battle had been evenly matched. Now he knew why they didn't encounter the victors slinking away. Either that or the survivors who could move had run without taking trophies. Cashing in a severed head wasn't worth it if it meant losing your own. These men fought for something; Sorrow was only there for money, not glory. He walked through the scene, looking at corpses. A hand reached out and grabbed his pants.

"Mercy," the man whispered. His face was pale, and blood spurted from his lips. An arrow stuck out of his belly. Black blood seeped around the wooden shaft with every breath, coating his hand that tried to keep it in.

Liver shot, Sorrow thought, knowing the black blood was a fatal hit. This man would die and die slowly.

"Please, some water." More blood, this bright red, bubbled from his lips.

Sorrow turned as Fin came and stood over the man, straddling him. He had a wicked grin on his face and his sword in hand.

"Mercy, you say," Fin said, pointing the sword at the man's heart.

The man's labored breath increased, causing the arrow to shudder and him to wince.

Fin didn't wait for a response. He touched the tip of his blade to the man's chest and slowly pushed.

Sorrow watched, waiting for the young man to thrust, delivering the fatal blow. He didn't. Slowly, the blade descended, piercing clothing and flesh. Ribs groaned and cracked beneath the blade as more blood rose.

"Ah," the man moaned. He let go of Sorrow's leg and the arrow and grabbed at the sword blade. This wasn't mercy.

Fin bared his teeth and pushed harder. The honed edges of his sword sliced through the man's palms, cutting them deeply. He reached the man's ribs and had to put a little more weight behind his push. The sword cracked and separated bone, finally reaching the fluttering heart.

The soldier was crying, and more blood rushed from his mouth, making him gag. Finally, he was dead.

Sorrow stared. Not at the dead man, but at Fin.

Fin pulled his sword from the man's chest. He looked up at Sorrow and smiled. This one wasn't forced, it was genuine. Without a word, Fin turned and looked for another wounded man with which to wet his blade.

Zakkas walked over to Sorrow, watching Fin scour the area for more wounded men to kill. He held a bloody, curved knife. "There is something off about that boy," Zakkas said. "Something dark in his eyes. In the Land of the Burning Sands, the Sultan keeps an army of boys like him. Dark, soulless boys, who are ready to kill at a whim. They are the most feared amongst our people, and it looks like we have one in our midst."

Sorrow grunted, but didn't speak. There was no need to. Was he that soulless killer when he was young? He wanted to deny it, saying all the men and women he killed along the way were justified, but were they? His quest to become a blade master was long and bloody. It was a debt of gold and gore, one that he repaid in the fighting pits around the world, finally ending him in Kresh'i, where he was destined to die. But he didn't die, no, he took life. One by one, veterans, gnarled warriors came up against the young boy with dark hair and a snake tattoo. They laughed at him and offered him a quick death, but were left staring at the fading sun as their life ebbed away. And for what? To repay a debt, or was it because Sorrow loved it? The rush of the crowd, the danger of dodging a blow, or feeling a blade enter you, knowing a matter of inches could end your life. It was all of it. When he stayed in the pits after his debt was repaid, he knew his soul was in jeopardy. Sorrow may not have loved the Church, but he certainly believed in his soul. Everything in the world had one, and his was as dark as pitch. Almost as black as the ink on his skin.

One by one, wounded men were executed, mostly with a quick slice to the throat. That was, unless Fin got to them first. The men that were already turned into meat, were dragged over to a waiting log, where Jagrim stood ready with his axe.

Jagrim aimed at a young man who had died from an arrow in the throat and swung. His blade cut through flesh and bone, burying itself into the bloody wood. The head of the young man fell, being grabbed up by another. Quickly and without ceremony, it was stuffed into a sack. The headless corpse was pushed away, left to roll down the embankment, landing with a meaty slap on the stones below.

"Damn, who knew head-lopping would be such hard work?" Jagrim said. He wiped his sweaty brow with the back of his hand, leaving a smear of blood that almost matched the color of his hair. He smiled, knowing each head was money, and this trip had been his idea. "Next," he said.

Soon, the burlap sacks were wet and dripping, full of severed heads. It was a good haul, more than enough for their first encounter.

The sun was low and out of sight, leaving a red streak across the sky in the west. The last body had been desecrated.

"Back to the camp?" Jagrim asked Sorrow. He was wiping down his axe and knew he'd have to spend a few hours with a whetstone. His shoulders ached, but in a good way.

Sorrow nodded. They had just enough light to traverse the mountainside back to their campsite. None of them wanted to spend the night surrounded by stinking guts. Besides, they knew many carrion creatures came out in the darkness to feed.

"Alright, you dogs, back to the camp. Tomorrow, we cash in these stinky, fucking things." Jagrim put his foot on a sack of heads.

CHAPTER 11

It stalked the mountains like the apex predator it was. Its skin was dark, like the earth it came from. On four legs, it skittered over fallen boulders and trees. Those four legs, each ending in a flurry of claws, grabbed the trunk of the tallest tree. With an unnatural nimbleness, it climbed. The smell of human meat was strong, flooding the slits it had for a nose. Its six eyes, all balanced on crustacean-like stalks, scanning. The sunlight was foreign to it, but it made do, adapting to feed. Since it had been awakened, it was hungry. The man-flesh it had already consumed was delectable, a taste that it hadn't experienced in generations. It salivated, leaving a clear trail of saliva dripping down the tree. Its mouth, its horrible mouth, was underneath it, where the belly of a *normal* four-legged beast would be. This was by design, allowing it to watch for threats as it fed. The clawed legs could shove meat into the hellish maw, while the eyes swiveled toward more prey or even danger.

The nostrils of the ancient evil expanded and took in the coppery scent of human blood and viscera. It was a heady bouquet, smelling like a perfect meal to the beast.

The light of the horrid sun was almost gone, making the sky look like blood; a favorite. The six eyes blinked, relaxing as the sun dipped below the horizon. Another gust of wind and another, more potent scent of blood. Its tongue hung from its mouth, tasting the air, discerning where the scent was coming from. It wasn't certain, but it had a direction...and hunger.

The creature climbed down the tree, leaving deep gouges in the rough bark. It moved with lithe grace over the rocky terrain as if it were on a flat field. Closer, stronger, the smell of blood drove it forward. The hunger was intense, gnawing at its gut, urging it on. Urging it to feed.

The sky was a deep shade of purple, but to it, it was perfect. The eyes darted around, seeking what its nose had already detected. It plunged down a bluff, digging its claws into the rocky earth to slow its descent. The scene before it was a feast of gore.

Bodies of humans lay scattered. They were dead, which didn't matter, even though living meat was better. The beast growled in happiness and skittered over to the first headless corpse. The clawed feet ripped and tore, pulling stiff flesh from the body. Its mouth opened wide, accepting the gift of cold meat. Bones were snapped and shoved into the chasm, being turned into mush by the rows of teeth.

Darkness settled over the Borderlands. The

full moon was covered by the fat clouds in the sky, casting long shadows on the mountains. The beast didn't need light to feed, in fact, it preferred darkness. In the inky black of night, the sound of flesh ripping echoed off the stones.

Jagrim's whetstone hissed along the dull edge of his axe. The head chopping had beat the blade up, but nothing a good sharpening couldn't handle.

The men had a few small fires burning, all of which were close by. They were still in an active battle zone, so sentries were set along the edge of the light.

After their stop in Ayr, a lot of the men had left or just never returned to the ship. They didn't mention any reason, but Sorrow knew his use of blood magic was probably to blame. That, and his willingness to cut the throat of a holy man without the blink of an eye. That was one thing he wished he could've taken back. Not because he harbored any guilt over killing Vicar Prentas or Brother Kirsh, but what he'd discovered among the Vicar's personal properties. The dark dealings of the Church, whether or not they were true. Who was involved and to what extent? Maybe the Vicar would've seen they were on the same side and dismissed the charges. But, more than likely, not.

He didn't much care about the other men who'd left. With the terrain of the Borderlands, they were better off without them. The few that stuck with him, besides Jagrim's men, were the best of the lot, anyway. They were the cutthroats, gamblers, killers, or men that didn't give a fuck about morals, but followed the sound of coins. Those were the men he needed next to him in a war-zone.

Sorrow sat next to Jagrim on a log. His sword didn't take any damage in the hills, but he drew it anyway.

Jagrim watched Sorrow from the corner of his eye, neither man talking, but both men knew what the other was thinking: Fin. They'd each seen the looks on the faces of their men, watching Fin slaughter the wounded soldiers without mercy. It was the job, but one that needed to be done quickly and efficiently.

Sorrow took an oiled cloth from his pack and wiped his sword down in the shimmering firelight.

"Has he always been that way?" Sorrow asked, not needing to mention a name.

Jagrim spat on his axe head and rubbed at a stubborn stain. He used the saliva for lubrication and kept sharpening.

"Aye, the boy's head has never been right." Jagrim put his axe across his knees and leaned closer to Sorrow. "He's got a black heart, that boy does, but he's a killer in combat. No fear and knows when to strike. With a little sword talent," he pointed to the black snake tattooed on Sorrow's hand, "he could be a force to be reckoned with."

Sorrow clenched his right hand, making the

snake curl up. The snake that told the world of his skills with a blade. The snake he never truly wanted.

"And then maybe the boy would stop talking to himself," Jagrim said.

A memory flashed in Sorrow's mind of weeks earlier, when he and Jagrim had come back to the inn after an unsuccessful night of trying to find female company. Standing outside of Fin's room, listening to the boy talking. At first, he thought Fin was talking to himself, like Jagrim had said, but when he heard the other voice—the strange, almost ethereal voice—, he knew it wasn't true. There was someone else in that room, of that Sorrow was certain. But something didn't sound *right* about them. No, it was off, like they were talking from down the hall, not as if they were standing in the same room. Sorrow didn't know why, but he kept that to himself. Even though he knew Fin had a dark side, Sorrow felt a connection with the boy. It was a connection he wished he'd had with a mentor when he was his age. His mentor wasn't much of a guiding light, forcing him into combat and eventually pushing him to get the tattoo that was laid upon his hand. His mentor only saw dollar signs in young Sorrow, not a friend or companion.

"I'm not sure that boy needs any help in the killing department." The sight of Fin killing the wounded men was still fresh in his mind. Not to mention what the fat man had said before Fin killed him. About the whores—the girls found raped and mutilated.

"Well, ye wanted killers and ye got killers, especially with that one." Jagrim gave his axe one last look. The edge was sharp again and ready to cut more flesh. "Let's just be happy his blade is going into the enemies and not us." Jagrim stood and put his axe back on his belt. He stretched to a symphony of cracking vertebrae. "I'm gonna piss and get some of the shit food Zakkas made."

Jagrim walked over to another fire, saying something to Zakkas, and clapped the man on the shoulder. There was a grin, a laugh, and a bowl of food.

Sorrow wasn't hungry, he felt uneasy. He didn't know why, but he did. Wet work, killing, even begging men, had never bothered him. No, he had a strong resolve for murder; years in the fighting pits would do that to a man. There was something else that was niggling him. Like he had the tip of a knife in between his shoulder blades. It felt like he was being watched, as if there was something in the shadows, beyond the flickering firelight. Sorrow turned, expecting to see something, man, or beast, standing behind him, but it was only darkness.

Fin had eaten, but wasn't hungry. Still, he kept up appearances and ate and laughed. But something bothered him. It was something warm against his skin, willing him to gaze into it, to answer for what he'd done.

Jagrim had just come over to the fire to eat with them. The big man sat with a steaming bowl of food and let out a laugh. Fin was shocked at the playful nature of these men, especially knowing they were still in an active war zone. They flew no colors of either nation, but other mercs could be lurking nearby, ready to wipe out some of their competition with arrows from the dark.

Fin adjusted his shoulder blades, as if he could feel an arrow entering his flesh. The warmth was growing and not just in his belly from the spicy food.

The amulet was burning. He knew *she* wanted to talk to him. It was a conversation long coming and after their last one, Fin knew he needed to change his ways. When the Queen gives an order, it's to be followed. And he knew the consequences if not.

Fin set his bowl down and stood. "That was great, Zakkas," he said, holding his stomach. "But I don't think my guts were ready for all of those spices."

Zakkas laughed. "That is flavor, my pink-skinned friend."

"Aye, it's got some heat to it, but it's not nearly as shitty as usual," Jagrim said, stuffing a lump of seasoned, dry meat into his mouth. "Much better," he said. Flecks of food landed on his beard as he spoke.

The moon wasn't as bright as Fin would've liked, but it was enough to allow him to walk away from the encampment. Thanks to the massive boulders in the area, he didn't have to go very far for privacy. He knew where the scouts were, and there was no way they were walking up and down the hillside in the dark. He was the only one crazy enough to do that.

Fin looked around and listened. Nothing, just the sound of the night creatures, but nothing human stirred. He adjusted his cloak and draped it over his head so he was in total darkness. The amulet felt like a hot coal against his skin and he pulled it out from underneath his shirt.

The surface shined like it was in front of a bonfire. Glowing in the darkness, the metal shimmered and danced in Fin's hands. His heart raced as an image came to life. An image that many people had seen just before their deaths.

She was the Queen, his Queen. A female face that was all too familiar coalesced in metal, taking shape.

"My Queen," Fin muttered. "I hav—,"

"Silence," she said. "Do not speak to me until I permit you. Do you understand?"

Fin nodded, not daring to test her. Even from halfway around the world, he knew her powers could still reach him. They were powers that no man could fight. Powers granted by a dark god.

"You had one task in the vile city of Ayr and yet you still failed me. Why did you so easily disobey your Queen? Think about your answer, for it may be the last thing you utter."

Something shifted in the darkness. The urge

to throw the cloak off his head and draw his sword was nearly a physical manifestation. But he held still, working his answer over and over in his mind.

"I—I have tried, my Queen, but the men I'm with, they had other ideas. They wanted to leave Ayr and I know they're my only transport. They're my only way to being reunited with you."

"Bahh," she shrieked. "Lies. You know very little about me, boy. You only *think* you do, but in reality, you have the mind of a bug."

"I'm sorry, my Queen," Fin said, but the visage of the Queen didn't move. For a moment, he thought she may have been frozen in the metal.

"And what were you doing in Ayr if not completing the task I'd given you? The one fucking task you'd been sent to do?"

Fin gulped. Every night he was on the prowl for women, he was supposed to be hunting other targets: members of the Church. It was the one task she'd given to him: find loyalists to the Church of the Refining Light and kill them. Kill them and any and all members that were loyal to *their* god. But, Fin had other perversions, other blood lusts to fulfill. He didn't think their time in Ayr would end so abruptly, but again, that could be perceived as his fault.

"I've failed you," Fin said. There was no use in telling her the truth; he had a feeling she already knew.

"Yes, you have. But, I would be a horrible leader if I threw away such a valuable piece of my puzzle. Your role is far from over and the murders of the Church scum were only a test. A test in which you failed. Even the Church man on your ship you failed to kill."

"Another man—Sorrow—killed him before he could taste my blade. Please, you must believe me."

Again, the Queen paused. Even in the metal, she looked elegant and deadly. Something flashed over her face, but only for a split second. Her brow scrunched and her eyes were slits. "Sorrow?" she asked. Another word rose on her lips, but she quelled it immediately.

"Yes, he's a ruffian, a slave that we found washed ashore. He used blood magic to kill the—" he paused, not knowing what he should say about the necromancer, "—necromancer."

The Queen nodded. "That was not only a 'necromancer, but a servant of Xziris."

"Yes, yes, my apologies. The vicar and his acolyte took offense to this use of magic, even though it saved their lives. When they tried to take him into custody..." he just let it drift off. There was no need to go into more detail.

"And where is your next destination?" she asked.

"I do not yet know, my Queen, but I will contact you immediately."

"Yes, you will. Things are moving quickly and ever-growing, and your obedience is required or so help me, your death will be things of nightmares."

"I understand," Fin said, but was talking to no one. The amulet winked out like a fire that had been doused. His heart was racing as he slowly removed the cloak. A part of him expected to see her standing in front of him. A monster in the darkness, made of shadow and black magic, but he was alone.

Or at least, he thought.

CHAPTER 12

It had eaten, filling its belly with the cold flesh of dead corpses, but it wanted more. It wanted blood and brain, warm viscera, not the cold guts it had consumed. Spoiled by the flesh of the living, it only craved that. It lived to feed, getting its fill until once again it could find a dark hole in which to rest.

A fresh smell, mixed with old, blew on the night breeze: smoke and man. It wasn't the smell of dead men, no; it was the fresh scent of living meat. Of warm blood pumping through live bodies. It flexed its clawed feet, scoring stone. The beast itched with the anticipation of feeling death, like it had first felt when the men invaded its cave. The feeling of hot flesh surrendering under the sharpness of the claws and the pop it made when shoved into its mouth. The crunch of their skulls and texture of their brains.

More drool, this time mixed with dried blood, dripped from the mouth of the foul beast. It was still hungry, and it knew another meal was waiting in the darkness.

Wrorch leaned against a tree, looking into the gloom around their camp. He was one of the few men who stuck it out with Sorrow after he'd killed the vicar. There wasn't much of a choice as far as he was concerned. He was wanted by authorities in almost every major city and had thought it wise to stay aboard the ship. As badly as he wanted to explore Ayr, he knew he wouldn't be able to control his urges. And one attentive guardsman would have sent him right to the executioner without question. Crime was a way of life for him, and he was good at it. Whether it was burglary, arson, assault, rape, or murder, Wrorch had done it. There was no principle in it. He did it to get paid, plain and simple. In most instances, he enjoyed his work, sometimes a little too much.

And it was time for him to take the first watch for the night. He expected little combat in the dark, but having a good perimeter was the best way to not get your throat slit in your bed. On their trek into the mountains, they'd seen a few other roving bands of men and women, but they were never close enough. When they landed at the docks of the Borderlands, it was quite obvious there would be competition in these hills. What better way to cash in than to kill your rivals at night, and steal the heads they've already collected?

Wrorch picked at his nails. He bit into a

stubborn sliver, tasting dried blood, and spat.

The light of the full moon was hidden behind fat clouds, but they were moving out. Soon, the mountainside would be bathed in silvery light. His watch was almost up anyway, but at least he wouldn't have to strain his eyes much longer.

It was as if someone had lit a lantern. The clouds moved, exposing the silvery moon, and making the entire mountainside look like a strange world.

He scratched his back against the tree, gazing into the night.

He froze; his eyes locked on a boulder. A boulder that was moving. A boulder with four long legs.

"What the fuck?" Wrorch put his hand on his sword, half-drawing it from the sheath. His eyes stayed locked on the massive shape. It moved over the rocks and trees like a spider. Shadows danced over it, and, in the moonlight, six eyes glimmered. He had been in many fights, killed many men and been badly wounded twice, but never in his life had he been this terrified. He was scared, but knew he had a job to do. Wrorch put his fingers in his mouth to sound an alarm, but his brain was barely registering. Spittle wet his hand, but that was it.

The creature, which was moving slowly, stalking, burst forward. He yanked his fingers from his mouth and drew his sword.

The monster was on him in seconds, reaching with its clawed legs, and grabbing at him. Wrorch avoided the first attack, sidestepping the razor-sharp appendages. He had seen nothing like the beast and didn't know where to strike. Normally, he'd try to decapitate something of such size, but there was no discernable head, only eyes and a slit for a nose. The body of the beast was large and made as good of a target as anything. Stones shifted underneath him, and he prepared his footing for a thrust. Two of the six eyes turned, looking to see where he'd gone, but they were too late. Wrorch stabbed and stabbed hard.

His sword struck the flesh of the beast and snapped. He stared for a moment, thinking he'd buried the blade deep into the flank of the monster, but the skin was unblemished. The monster could've been made of stone.

A clawed leg snapped out and grabbed Wrorch's sword arm, which was still holding the broken blade. With a quick twist, his arm was snapped as he was yanked forward. He opened his mouth to scream, but another clawed appendage closed over his face. The claws dug into his skull as he was pushed to the ground and pulled in. He'd dropped the broken sword and reached up to fight against the claw, but it was no use. He was being drawn in. Hot breath washed over his face and for an instant, the claw moved, and he could see.

He saw teeth.

CHAPTER 13

Sorrow slept, but barely. He was never a heavy sleeper, something he attributed to his childhood spent in the orphanage of the Church. The older boys and some of the Brothers were absolute nightmares to the younger ones. Late-night attacks for perceived slights during the day were commonplace. Some boys would go to sleep thinking they'd had a pretty good day. That was until they were awoken by fists, or wet cloths thrown over their faces. Usually, it was both, as their arms and legs were pinned down, making any resistance nearly impossible.

Sorrow was dreaming, and in his mind, he could hear something wet. It sounded like a pig of a man, chewing with his mouth open. In his mind's eye, he could almost see it, his brain creating the slob cramming food into his gullet. Slowly, his body fought against the dream and his eyelids flicked open.

Nothing. There was no one chewing near him. Just the flickering fire and humps of sleeping men. The night was quiet...too quiet.

Just like when they'd entered the realm of the

necromancer.

Sorrow threw his blanket off him and sat up. He clenched his sword and looked around as he stood.

Jagrim, one of the sleeping lumps near him, roused from his friend's urgent awakening.

"Wh—what is it?" Jagrim was half-asleep, but looking around for something to punch. His axe was next to him and his hands fumbled in the dirt for it.

Sorrow put a finger to his lips, quieting the man. "Listen," Sorrow said.

Jagrim stood, clenching his axe. The freshly sharpened blade shone in the firelight. He looked around, noticing the full moon was finally out, bathing the landscape in an ethereal glow.

"Aye, what the fuck is that? It sounds like Gortul at the dinner table, but bigger." He looked at Sorrow. "Much fucking bigger."

Sorrow squinted, gazing into the gloom. "What the fuck is that?" Something moved in the distance amongst the boulders and trees. Something massive.

Jagrim watched the monstrosity move towards them and his mind flashed back to the flesh hulk the necromancer had created. "I hope ye have another fireball up yer arse again, Sorrow." He licked his lips, pushing strands of his bushy beard from his mouth. "Cause it looks like we're gonna need it." Without waiting for an answer, Jagrim whistled three times and yelled. "To arms! To arms! To arms!"

The men jumped up. They looked around in

panic, expecting an attacker to be amongst them. Blades were drawn and each man's head spun, looking for a target or threat.

"Who was the sentry in the east?" Sorrow asked. He knew most of the men, but a few of them he was still leery of.

Jagrim thought for a moment and said, "Wrorch."

"Well, I assume he's dead." Sorrow watched the monster stalk towards them.

The moonlight was bright, bright enough to give them a glimpse of the nightmare approaching them.

It was huge and walked on four clawed legs. The body of the monster was the size of a large cow, but there was no discernable head. Six eye stalks rose off the front of it, and just below that was a nose slit, which was opening and closing. The beast didn't rush them. Instead, it stalked forward, feeling them out.

That made Sorrow even more nervous; it was smart, not a mindless hulk of meat.

"What in the blue fuck is that thing?" Gortul asked. He was shirtless and holding his mace.

"I'm not sure, but I think we're about to find out," Sorrow said, watching the creature enter the camp.

It was worse in the firelight. Its body was dark, like it was made from the earth. The eyes, which seemed to constantly be moving, were wide and almost lidless. They were dark and searching.

The slit below the eyes was sniffing like it was a dog, breathing in their scent. Its legs were spider-like, ending in a clawed foot.

Claaven, one man near the furthest fire, had a spear in his hand. He looked around for help, but realized his fire mates had fallen back with the other men. He was wild-eyed, but ready to fight. He'd take the glory for himself and kill the beast while the other men cowered. His time in the Paldashian army had made him a formidable spearman, and he was ready to put his skills on display.

"Come get it, you fucking cunt!" Claaven yelled, keeping his eyes trained on the beast, which now had a lock on him. His spear wasn't too long, but long enough and better than closing with a sword. He didn't know if the monster had a brain, but in all his years of killing, he found it best to aim for the face. Not that there was much of a face, but the eyes would do.

The creature skittered forward with a burst of speed, right into range of Claaven's spear.

He thrust out, his attack going wide. The honed metal tip of the spear slammed hard into the beast. Claaven had a smile on his face, waiting for that rewarding feeling of steel and wood entering flesh, but it never came. The tip of the spear skipped off the skin of the beast, not even leaving a scratch. Claaven stood in shock as a clawed foot snapped the head of the spear off like it was kindling.

"Fuck," Sorrow muttered, watching the battle, which was about to end.

Another of the claws shot forward and grabbed Claaven by the stomach. The man screamed and thrashed as the hellish claws pierced his gut. Using its back legs, the creature rose, exposing the gaping hole in its stomach full of teeth.

Claaven's screams turned to childlike shrieks of fear and pain, as he was drawn towards the drooling mouth. A long tongue wrapped around his neck, like it was the body of a constrictor, and pulled.

The stench was almost unbearable, and if his death wasn't imminent, he would've vomited.

Thousands of teeth, all shapes and sizes, coming from different angles, closed around Claaven's skull. His brain popped like a log being split and the teeth ground together like stone, pulping it all together.

An arrow flew from the men, this too bouncing off the seemingly impenetrable hide of the monster.

It dropped the headless corpse of Claaven on the ground. Blood oozed from the stump of his neck. The creature now had new meals to consume, and it was still hungry.

"Fire! Get fire," Sorrow said, still with his eyes locked on the monster. The men, who were almost entranced by the slaughter of one of their comrades, scattered. They grabbed torches from their packs and snapped pine branches from above.

The creature made a shrill sound, almost like wind through a tunnel, and rushed forward, straight at Sorrow.

He gripped his blade with two hands, wondering if he should try his luck with steel against the abomination.

The monster crouched low, adding a burst of speed as it struck out with its claws.

Sorrow parried the attack with the flat of his blade and rolled away. The stones and hard earth scraped his back, but that was the furthest thing on his mind. He snapped up, blade at the ready, as the creature returned, continuing the onslaught.

The beast swiped at Sorrow and he saw a chance for a strike, hoping the heavy steel of his blade would damage the legs of the monster.

Sorrow ducked the attack, rising under the beast, right where one leg was attached to the body. He swung up, not the most powerful strike in a sword attack, aiming for the inner joint. His blade hit...and skidded right off. Again, he moved away, avoiding the deadly claws.

"The fucking fire! Now!" Sorrow yelled, sword at the ready.

His men rushed forward with blazing torches and branches. The creature hissed again, unleashing a faucet of bloody drool from its mouth, but it didn't run.

"Ah, take that, ya fucking cunt!" Jagrim leaped in, shoving his torch closer to the thing's eyes.

The stalky eyes snapped shut as the fire found its flesh. Flames danced over the hide of the beast, blackening it. The creature thrashed in pain, but the damage was minimal.

The men, now seeing the monster could be hurt, closed in.

Enraged and in pain, the hellish beast flailed, whipping its front legs out.

Yon, one of the few stragglers that had stayed with Sorrow, was in the path of one of those clawed appendages. Yon raised his sword to block the attack, hoping to deflect the claws away so he could strike. He'd never faced strength like what was in front of him. The monster's leg smashed into the sword, pushing it like it wasn't even there. The edge of the blade shot back, firmly wedging itself into Yon's skull. His bone cracked as the blade buried itself into his brain, splitting him like a ripened melon. Yon fell dead in a heap.

The other men dropped back, gasping at the strength of the monster in front of them. They were killers, through and through, but killers of men. Very few of them, until they'd faced the necromancer, had fought a creature as powerful as the one in front of them.

Jagrim's torch flickered. But he had fallen back as well. "Aye, this fucking thing is going to slaughter us," he said to Sorrow.

Sorrow watched the monster stalk closer. A look of hatred danced across the six eyes. He knew his friend was right. They had to kill it or try to escape it in the dark mountainside. It was suicide either way. He gripped his sword tight and even the snake tattoo, which usually had a thirst for blood, was silent.

Zakkas had his curved sword in hand, but he knew it was useless against the monster. Steel wouldn't kill the beast, but...

"Silver," he shouted. The men looked at him like he was crazy. In the background, the monster hissed as more flaming torches were thrust at it, but they were dwindling. No man since Yon had tried attacking with a weapon. "My grandmother used to tell us stories of beasts that would live in the desert. Monsters of legend that would feast on trading caravans and were unkillable unless you had magic or silver." He scanned the men, his eyes landing on Fin, who was waving a burning pine bough at the monster's face. "Fin, give me that knife."

Fin heard his name, but in his distraction, just barely avoided a lethal swipe from the beast. He stepped back, hoping another man would take his place.

"What?" Fin asked, trying to look back at Zakkas from the corner of his eye. Embers rose from his torch, lifting into the night sky, escaping the murder scene.

"Your knife, the silver one. Give it here." Zakkas sheathed his sword and looked around. A snapped spear shaft sat discarded on the ground. He picked it up, hoping it was long enough.

Fin threw his torch at the monster, watching it bounce off the impenetrable skin. He pulled the knife from his belt.

It was simple, even for an expensive blade.

The knife shimmered in the firelight, but the flames danced differently for silver. For a moment, Fin hesitated, knowing his money would be long gone. He knew there was no point in having money if you were dead.

Zakkas held his hands out, waiting for Fin to throw him the knife. "Throw it here!" Zakkas clapped his hands. The beast ripped another man's head off, stuffing it into its maw. Over the din of battle, the sounds of the skull being devoured echoed through the mountains.

Fin gripped the handle and lofted the knife to Zakkas. It flew end over end, and with a deft hand, Zakkas snatched it from the air.

Zakkas kneeled and cut a piece of his shirt off in a long strip.

"Now's not the time for arts and crafts," Jagrim said.

Zakkas ignored the man and fastened the knife to the shaft, making a spear. He checked his bindings, hoping they were good enough; their lives depended on it.

"Distract that thing so I can get close without getting my fucking head taken off," Zakkas said, giving the spear a practice thrust. It wasn't quite military issue, but it would do...he hoped.

Sorrow saw the makeshift spear, and the idea clicked in his mind. *Silver!* He should've known.

"Jagrim, rip down another branch, and let's see if we can give him a chance to get in close and end this."

Jagrim thought both men were crazy, but he'd done some baffling things in his time as well. Without another word, he swung his axe into the low-hanging pine branches, severing a few.

Sorrow didn't wait; he snatched one right away and dipped it into the nearest fire. The pine needles lit and crackled, catching the wood on fire. Sorrow didn't like the idea of rushing the monster with a flaming stick, but they were out of options. He ran forward, waving his torch.

The creature recoiled as the fire was pushed into its face. Quickly, it swiped, narrowly missing Sorrow, who ducked the blow. The gust of wind from the strike made the flames dance, but they held, even growing brighter. Six eyes moved around, looking for more targets. Men skipped around the monster, waving flame, but none got close enough to let the fire do any damage. The corpse of Yon, which was mangled from being trampled by boots and claws, was still fresh in their minds.

Zakkas moved on the creature's flank, hoping to find a spot to jam the silver blade home. The eyes of the beast, at least two of them, followed him, watching his every move. He avoided a strike, dancing away from the blow.

Sorrow watched his flame flicker as the pine was consumed. They were running out of options. Zakkas needed to move and hurry, or they'd all die. Sorrow had an idea, but he didn't know if it was brilliant or suicidal. He backed out of the fray, leaving the last few men with torches to maintain the beast.

Sorrow grabbed his pack and upended it on the ground, looking for a jar, a small jar. He wished it was more blood magic, but it wasn't. It was something much simpler.

He grabbed it and put the cork in his mouth. The oil had little smell. It was neutral, the best kind for oiling a blade to keep it safe from rust. Sorrow pulled the cork with his teeth and drew his sword. He dumped the jar all over his blade, coating it. He thrust his steel into the fire and took a step back.

With a *whoosh,* his sword immolated. Liquid flame dripped from it and he kept it level so as not to burn himself. He looked like a hero from the legends as he moved forward toward the monster.

The surrounding men saw the flaming weapon and stepped away.

Sorrow had the attention of the beast, which was still trying to pin down Zakkas. He waded into combat. Hopefully not for the last time.

The first strike came unexpectedly low. He parried it, shuffling back, but immediately moved forward. His flaming sword met flesh. The steel didn't penetrate, but the flames brought a shriek from the beast. The monster, more aggravated than wounded, struck again. This attack was straight on and meant to kill. Sorrow spun, deflecting the clawed appendage with the flat of his sword. Off balance from the powerful attack, Sorrow thrust forward, right at the gigantic eyes. His jaw was clenched as he willed his blade to enter the monster's hide. Sorrow's strike was true; his blade hit its mark, but again, only the fire did any kind of damage.

Zakkas almost forgot why he was standing there. Sorrow's swordplay was like a dance as he dipped and struck the beast with cat-like grace. His flaming blade leading the way.

"Stick it already!" Jagrim yelled. He, too, along with the other men, watched the fight.

Zakkas snapped out of his trance and moved forward. He didn't know where the monster was the weakest, but he didn't care. He was going to put the blade deep into its flesh.

Sorrow parried another attack, but the flame was dying on his blade. It was now or never.

Zakkas had his moment. The creature, knowing the flame was almost gone, reared up on its back legs, attacking with both front ones. Zakkas rushed forward and stabbed.

He was expecting there to be resistance, seeing what the other blades had done against the monster, but there was none. It was like putting a freshly sharpened sword into a rotting carcass. The silver punched through and punched through deep.

The monster shrieked and screamed. It fell to the ground, thrashing and kicking up dirt and mud —mud made from the blood of men. It rolled onto its back, trying to push the blade free, but only driving it deeper. The horrid mouth was on full display in the firelight. A gaping, circular mouth, lined with hellish teeth, cried a death wail. Finally, the beast lay still, slain.

Sorrow rubbed his sword on the ground, extinguishing what was left of the weak flame. He was panting, but still smiled at Zakkas, who was looking at him.

"Maybe, next time, do that sooner," Sorrow said. Sweat fell from his brow and he wiped his face with the back of his sleeve. His heart was finally slowing to a normal pace. The surrounding men relaxed, lowering their weapons but not sheathing them.

Zakkas' white teeth shone bright in the moonlight. "Why, you were doing a fine job."

Sorrow nodded and inspected his sword. It would need some work, but it was still usable. Jagrim walked over to him as he was sheathing his blade.

"Triple the sentries and rotate every hour. I want no more surprises," Jagrim barked. "Keep small fires and let us pray there aren't any more of these fucking things roaming around." The men, not wanting to be around the disgusting corpse of the monster, quickly split into groups and headed out into the darkness. "Aye, how much do ye think we'll get for that one?" Jagrim put his meaty arm around Sorrow's shoulders and pointed at the dead monster.

"Not sure, but I hope it's a lot. Either way, I think our time in the Borderlands is over. Wouldn't you agree?"

"Aye, I think that's a great idea, my friend." Jagrim slapped him on the back and walked over to inspect the dead beast. His mind was seeing bags of gold.

The remaining men, who weren't on watch, began gathering their dead. A funeral pyre would have to be constructed in the morning unless they left their carcasses for the carrion creatures. Sorrow had a feeling he knew what would happen. His band of men had again been reduced, but that was more profit for the survivors. Fires crackled and flickered, casting shadows in the night. Sorrow still had a feeling of unease, even though the creature lay dead in front of him. He didn't know why, but it felt as if an arrow was aimed at his back. Slowly, as not to disturb the men on corpse duty, he turned.

Fin stared at him, his sword still in hand. The boy's dark eyes shifted to look past Sorrow, but he'd seen the glare when he turned.

"You can sheath that," Sorrow said, pointing at Fin's blade.

Fin looked down as if he didn't know what Sorrow was talking about. He was startled to see the steel in his fist as if he were listening to something far away and dreaming.

"Oh, right," Fin said. He put his blade into the leather sheath. "I guess I'll take a guard post too." Without another word, Fin walked towards one of the small fires that had sprung up on their perimeter.

Sorrow watched him melt into the darkness. It was still the early hours of the morning and the sky had yet to lighten, but Sorrow knew there was no more sleep to come. He knew if he slept, his rest would be plagued with visions of monsters. Monsters on four legs…and two.

THE SECOND
INTERLUDE

Fucking Jagrim.

I have cut off many heads in my day, but I will never go headhunting again. While it sounded like a great idea from the beginning, it ended up costing lives. Yes, we made some coin from the stinking bags full of heads, but in the end, we lost a few men to the beast in the mountains.

That beast was something I'd never seen before, and I've been around. I've even killed a few 'so-called' monsters, but never that close to civilization. They were usually on the outskirts of small towns, such as with the cursed necromancer. But that was the first time I had to worry about a beast like that and human enemies lurking in the shadows. Not to mention my legs are quite sore from the mountainous terrain. If it weren't for Zakkas and Fin, we'd all be dead and eaten.

The following morning, we discussed what to do with the carcass of the beast. It was massive and even more terrifying in the daylight, but ultimately, we left it. There was no head to cut off and even in death, its tough hide proved formidable to our steel. And we were fresh out of silver knives. Fin never recovered his twice-stolen blade from the beast, but I think he was okay with that. And if he wasn't, fuck him. He was the main reason for us being in that cursed mountain range. He, and of course, Jagrim's big idea. If we didn't have to flee from Ayr like a band of fugitives, we would've been able to discuss our next destination and not rush to a war zone. There were talks about making port near to Ayr, but with quick birds and arcane devices, we wanted to clear the coast and move across the sea.

Again, Fin remains on my mind. The boy is a fighter, I'll give him that, but he's like a wild dog. He needs to either be broken or put down. There is no in-between for him. I have no qualms with him killing the fat man behind the tavern. That is a fight I've found myself in many times before. And the rush of a close-quarters duel is like nothing else. Feeling your blade sink into an enemy, delivering the killing blow...Anyway, the allegations about the duel caused me concern. It was no secret that women were being killed around the city. Jagrim and I knew firsthand, as finding a whore was difficult and expensive. I also know that many things are embellished the more times they're passed along. Such as the manner in which these women were killed. But that the fat man witnessed Fin with one of the girls before she was killed has given me a reason to pause. Many other men, those not hawking stolen Church goods, found menial jobs while in Ayr. They would return often smelling of their profession, requiring laundering of their clothes. Some men didn't care about the odors, nor who they offended with them. And then there was Fin. His dark cloak came back stinking and crusted with blood on more than one occasion. And yes, when questioned, he would tell us he'd taken up a position at an abattoir. But we've been around blood. Human blood and animal blood differ. Any man who's been in combat or taken a life knows the difference in that smell.

I didn't pry, and truly didn't care. The boy was a killer, so what? I was as well and at his age, with sword talent, I looked for a fight. I was the one in the streets feigning intoxication so thugs would try to jump me. With a quick draw of my sword—the snake tattoo wrapped around the hilt—I'd leave them bleeding in the streets. Sometimes I wouldn't kill them, but maim them for fun. A hard slash at their cocks, ensuring they'd never fuck or piss right again. A cut to the face, blinding them. Sometimes I'd test my accuracy and take off an ear, just to make sure I still had it.

I did.

When you spend years fighting and killing in dank pits for money and one day you're back in civilization, it can be tough. The rage I had built up over the years and the confidence with the blade—it was a deadly combination. And this was what I see in Fin. But I'm not so sure my young companion is out dueling men or picking fights with gangs. I saw it flash on his face when the fat man accused him. It was just a moment, but it was there. Had he been the one killing the girls? Or could it have been one, and he was being blamed for the rest? Hopefully, it was none and the fat man just felt slighted that a whore would rather fuck a young man, not a fat slob.

Time will tell, and as we sail across the sea once again, we have nothing but time. I will give Fin my attention and teach him, refine him, in the hopes he can find an outlet for the rage. The boy is a killer, that is a fact, but he's talented with the blade. Duels, not only to the death, are quite popular around the world. Nobility will often pay for the finest duelists, pitting them against each other in combat, using practice steels. This isn't nearly as much fun as bladed combat, but it can be a fine way to make a living. And if sometimes these nobles ask their duelist to perform some quiet wet work, it's usually followed by a hefty purse of gold.

Fin is a wild dog, and I will try to break him, to make him into a tame beast. And if I cannot, I will put him down.

ABOUT THE AUTHOR

Daniel J. Volpe

Daniel J. Volpe is an author of  extreme horror and splatterpunk. His love for horror started at a young age when his grandfather unwittingly rented him, "A Nightmare on Elm Street." Daniel has published with D&T publishing, Potter's Grove, The Evil Cookie Publishing, and self-published. He can be found on Facebook @ Daniel Volpe, Instagram @ dj_volpe_horror and Twitter @DJVolpeHorror . Signed books available at djvhorror.com

Other books by Daniel J. Volpe

Billy Silver
Awakened in Blood
Talia
Talia 2
A Gift of Death
Left to You
Only Psychos
Plastic Monsters
Sew Sorry (w Aron Beauregard)
Visceral 2 (w Patrick C. Harrison III)
Black Hearts and Red Teeth
Multiple Stab Wounds
A Story of Sorrow Book 1: Of Flesh and Blood

BOOKS IN THIS SERIES

A Story of Sorrow

Of Flesh And Blood

The Unburied

Fall To The Queen **Forthcoming**

Made in the USA
Middletown, DE
16 August 2023

36745408R00073